'I hope you have changed,' he said, taking her arm to guide her to the car.

Sensation shivered through her in a mixture of flame and ice. 'Why.'

'If you don't change you stagnate. I was a careless young fool with nothing but my own needs and desires in mind. You, of all people, should remember that. I'm not like that now.'

'I remember you being a leader—responsible and courageous and daring,' she said simply.

'Even when I made love to you and left you pregnant?' he asked with self-derisory contempt.

She glanced from her hands to his profile, an arrogant outline against the shimmering lights of the sea front. Screwing her courage to the sticking point, she said, 'You aren't Nick's father.'

His mouth tightened into a forbidding line. 'It won't work, Kate. I know his birth date—'

She interrupted jerkily, 'Patric, I tried to tell you before—you're not his father. Why would I lie to you?'

'I intend to find out.'

Robyn Donald has always lived in Northland in New Zealand, initially on her father's stud dairy farm at Warkworth, then in the Bay of Islands, an area of great natural beauty where she lives today with her husband and an ebullient and mostly Labrador dog. She resigned her teaching position when she found she enjoyed writing romances more, and now spends any time not writing in reading, gardening, travelling, and writing letters to keep up with her two adult children and her friends.

Recent titles by the same author:

FORBIDDEN PLEASURE
SURRENDER TO SEDUCTION

THE PATERNITY AFFAIR

BY
ROBYN DONALD

MILLS & BOON®

*First published in Great Britain 1999
Harlequin Mills & Boon Limited,
Eton House, 18-24 Paradise Road, Richmond, Surrey TW9 1SR*

© Robyn Donald 1999

ISBN 0 263 81663 X

*Set in Times Roman 10½ on 11 pt.
01-9905-54390 C1*

*Printed and bound in Norway
by AIT Trondheim AS, Trondheim*

CHAPTER ONE

OH, LORD, Kate Brown prayed silently. Oh, Lord, Oh, Lord, Oh, Lord, let this be over soon. *Please*. Beside her, her son let out an ecstatic yelp as the roller-coaster carriage swayed and dived, suspending them upside down for heart-shattering moments.

She forced her eyelids to open infinitesimally. While the world catapulted hideously around them she barked, 'Put your hands back on that bar! Now!'

'Oh, *Mummy*,' Nick protested, but obeyed.

Clamping her eyes shut again as the carriage went into another stomach-dropping spin, Kate thought wildly that his hands were long and tanned with tapered fingers—just like hers. In fact he looked so much like her that people often did a double take. Only *his* knuckles weren't white on the bar, and he didn't feel sick—his wide grin told her just how much he was enjoying himself.

Certainly he hadn't got his fearlessness—or whatever had made him wheedle until he finally got her onto the Triple-Loop Corkscrew Roller-Coaster—from her. That rash courage could have come from her parents, but she had no idea who'd bequeathed him his coaxing charm.

Not his father, she thought with a shudder. Remembering Nick's father was the worst thing to do when her stomach was already stressed to its maximum.

With the effortless ease of almost seven years' practice, she switched her mind into another channel, relaxing as the carriage steadied and slid quietly to a halt. Thank heaven it was over.

But when they were once more standing on solid ground

Nick, still fizzing, urged, 'Can we go again? Mummy, can we do it again? That was awesome.'

Never a truer word. Kate stared at him. 'Do you want to kill me?'

He grinned, blue-green eyes sparkling. 'You liked it really. I bet you did. And you'll like it much better if we go again now 'cause you'll know what's going to happen.'

'Once was quite enough, and anyway, Sea World is just about ready to close,' Kate said, steering him towards the exit. 'If you want a swim before dinner we have to go now. It gets dark early here.'

He threw her a disappointed glance, but said in a lordly tone, 'Well, all right.'

Kate laughed down at him. He beamed back, and she ruffled his black hair. As she withdrew her hand some atavistic sense, long asleep, set alarm bells clanging through her system. Turning, she met eyes—frigid iron-grey eyes—that swept her in a rapid, frightening scrutiny, then moved, inevitably, to the child at her side.

'Hello, Kate.' Patric Sutherland's voice was deadly.

Panic clutched her throat, stopped her brain. Dimly she heard Nick's startled exclamation, and then strong hands gripped her, holding her upright for a moment before settling her against a big, rock-solid body.

Enveloped in warmth, in the faint, evocative scent of male, she heard Patric say coolly, 'She'll be all right soon—she's just had a shock.'

Kate wrenched herself back from the longed-for oblivion of unconsciousness. Her deflated lungs filled on a gasping breath; she tried to pull herself away, but the arms around her remained unyielding.

Very quietly Patric said, 'Lean on me, Kate.'

'Nick,' she muttered desperately, stiffening herself against the dangerous haven of those arms.

'He's all right.'

But Nick said, 'Mummy?' with a betraying quiver.

Opening her eyes and blinking, Kate looked down at

her son, tall for a boy not yet six, and a little pale beneath his golden skin, his black hair with its red highlights setting off the blue-green eyes he shared with her.

Far too aware of the man who imprisoned her, she croaked, 'I must have been out in the sun too long.'

'I told you to wear your hat,' Nick pointed out, then added anxiously, 'Are you all right now?'

'Yes, of course.' She drew in a deep breath.

'Then why does he have to hold you up?'

'He doesn't any longer, because I'm perfectly able to stand up by myself,' she said, pulling back.

Patric released her, but kept one hand beneath her elbow, the long fingers deliberate and uncompromising. His touch, his closeness, seared through her, devastating her.

I have to get out of here!

The grimness in Patric's face might have been shock at this unwanted, unexpected meeting. Unfortunately a quick glance told her otherwise. Before she had time to react to the blaze of raw fury in his eyes, heavy lashes masked them, and when they lifted his gaze was opaque and unreadable.

'You need a drink,' he said brusquely. 'Come on, I'll get you one.'

Kate knew that look. She could object, protest, refuse, but she'd still find herself sitting in the coolness of a tea room drinking something. Patric always got his own way, and the seven or so years since she'd last seen him had chiselled more harshly a face already formidable at twenty-four. Then he'd been charismatic, irradiated by the promise of power; now it blazed forth—dominating and determined, intensely magnetic.

Someone—Fate perhaps, laughing cynically—had just walked over her grave.

Kate stretched out a hand to her son. After a swift look at the man who held her arm, Nick's hot fingers clamped onto hers. She squeezed and he squeezed back, the alarm in his face fading.

'Yes,' he said, nodding. 'That's what you need—a cup of tea.'

'All right,' she replied.

The few minutes it took to reach the café were barely enough to reinforce Kate's fragile composure. Where on earth had Patric come from? Was he living in Australia now? Here on the Gold Coast?

Impossible. Owner and managing director of one of New Zealand's most active and profitable aviation companies, he still lived in Auckland. The last newspaper article she'd read about him said that he also had a house in Aspen, Colorado, and apartments in London and New York.

Literally a jet-setter.

Once in the air-conditioned tea room, he held a chair for her, waiting until she was seated before signalling a waitress with a glance. Only Patric got such instant service, summoned by a combination of his physical presence— over six foot three of him, with broad shoulders and long legs—and something just as impressive but more intangible, the tough authority that stamped his face and bearing.

He asked, 'Tea or coffee, Kate?'

'Tea, thank you.'

'And what will you have?' Patric asked Nick.

'Orange juice or water, please,' he said politely.

Patric gave the order to the waitress, smiling at her as she tucked her pencil behind her ear. Kate had basked in that potent smile all through her adolescence; she didn't blame the waitress for blushing and simpering before hurrying off as though she'd been given a royal command.

No sign of the smile softened his angular features when he turned back to Kate. Unsparing eyes measured her, examining her face without any pretence at tact, then fell to her hand, noticing the lack of any wedding ring before flicking up again. 'Hello, Kate Brown,' he said silkily. 'The years have been kind to you—you're as beautiful as ever.'

ROBYN DONALD 9

'Thank you,' she said as she strove for a casual, friendly tone. It didn't work; all she could produce were stilted monosyllables. Repressing her churning emotions, she took a shallow breath and braced herself.

'Are you living in Australia now?' Patric asked, leaning back in his chair.

She couldn't lie, not with Nick sitting there. 'No.'

Sensing that Nick was about to break into speech, she gave him *the look*—the glare known to all children that means *not another word or there will be retribution.* Recognising it, Nick subsided into silence.

'So you're still a New Zealander?' Dark, metallic eyes were examining the mahogany highlights in her hair.

Almost seven years ago, on her eighteenth birthday— three days before he'd made love to her—he'd buried his face in her hair and told her never to cut it.

Did he remember? Yes, she thought feverishly as his gaze moved to her face, he remembered. Something brittle in her shattered, melted, dissolved.

'Yes.' And to cover the bluntness of her reply she tacked on, 'Do *you* live here?'

His beautiful, hard mouth twisted subtly. 'No. I'm over on business.'

Although beads of sweat clung stickily to her temples, and she couldn't dislodge a blockage in her chest, she managed to smile. 'It must be a pleasant place to work.'

'It depends on the business.' There was a cold, charged note in the deep voice when he asked, 'Aren't you going to introduce us?'

At first Kate's throat and mouth were too dry to get the words out. She had to swallow before she could say formally, 'This is my son, Nick. Nick, this is an old friend of mine, Mr Sutherland.'

Nick held out a hand. 'Hello, Mr Sutherland,' he said with solemn courtesy.

Patric's lean, bronzed fingers engulfed the slighter, boyish ones. Gravely he returned the greeting, and without pause asked, 'How old are you, Nick?'

'Six,' Nick said, adding before Kate could stop him, 'Well, not yet, but I will be soon. On the thirty-first of October—just five more weeks and then I'll really be six.'

Although Patric's gaze stayed on Nick, Kate didn't fool herself. Beneath the superb framework of that uncompromising face his brain was making connections. An exhausting mixture of despair and humiliation flowed through her. She was going to have to tell him, and that would effectively ruin the fantasy she'd hidden so well in the privacy of her mind that she hadn't even been aware of it until she saw Patric's ruthless, disturbing face again.

Welcome to the real world. Better late than never—but oh, it had hurt no one, that wistful little fairy story.

Patric said thoughtfully, 'You're tall for your age.'

'Yes.' Her son grinned, pleased at being the focus of Patric's attention. Nick could be reserved with strangers if he didn't like them, but he was no more immune to the charm of Patric's smile than anyone else. 'I'll soon be taller than Mummy. Mummy will be twenty-five in February next year, but Mr Frost says she looks like my sister, not my mother.'

Patric's smile was a masterpiece, establishing a men-together situation that had to appeal to a child with no visible father. 'Mr Frost is right. Who is he?'

'He's my teacher.'

This was getting too close to home. Clumsily, Kate interposed, 'What business brings you to the Gold Coast, Patric?'

His name stumbled across her tongue. For nearly seven long years it hadn't passed her lips, and saying it tore apart the barrier she'd constructed with such painful determination.

'I'm checking out a firm I'm thinking of buying,' he said pleasantly. 'What are you doing here?'

'She won a prize,' Nick told Patric importantly.

The waitress arrived then, with a tray. Kate accepted her tea gratefully, and drank some down.

But Nick hadn't finished. 'She made up a poem about lemonade, and so we got seven days in Surfers' Paradise and a free ticket to all the parks like this. We came now because it's the holidays. I have to go back to school when we get home.'

'I see,' Patric said. A rapier glance pierced Kate's meagre poise. 'Clever Kate.'

Nick visibly expanded, sitting straighter, taller. He asked, 'Have you got any boys like me, Mr Sutherland?'

Patric's expression froze. 'No,' he said, and added, 'I don't have a wife, you see. Mine died three years ago.'

Laura dead? 'I'm so sorry,' Kate said inadequately.

He said, 'It was a tragedy,' and looked again at Nick. 'Are you enjoying the theme parks?'

Nick beamed. 'Oh, yes,' he said eagerly, adding with a teasing glance at his mother, 'But Mummy doesn't like to go on the rides very much.'

'And you do?'

'I love them!' he said, with such exuberance that the people at the next table glanced at him and smiled.

Kate's heart contracted. That effortless magnetism had always surrounded her son; in his pram people used to stop and comment on what a splendid child he was. He'd gone sunnily through infancy to school, hiding his formidable intelligence and fierce will with a bright, open friendliness.

Patric's eyes lingered for a moment on Kate's hair. She just managed to stop herself from putting up a nervous hand to push the black tresses into shape, and her hand shook a little as she picked up her cup again.

He said lightly to Nick, 'I'm surprised you managed to persuade your mother onto a roller-coaster. She's always been afraid of heights.'

'I just asked and asked,' Nick told him, adding, 'Did you used to know Mummy? Is that why you came here?'

'I used to know her very well. When she was fourteen

she came with her uncle and aunt and cousins to live on
the big cattle and sheep station my father owned.'

'Tatamoa, in the Poto Valley?' Nick asked knowledge-
ably. 'She tells me stories about that place. One day we're
going to go there—when I'm bigger.'

Patric didn't look at Kate. 'Yes, that's it. Her uncle managed the station.'

'Did you live there too?'

Patric shook his black head. 'No, I lived in Auckland
with my parents, because my father worked there, but we
always came down for the summer holidays.'

'Did you see us on the roller-coaster?' Nick asked, with
the innocent self-absorption of the very young.

'Yes. I saw you from the hotel next door, and thought
it would be fun to say hello.'

Which seemed perfectly sensible to Nick. Nodding, he
drank his orange juice with enthusiasm. Kate kept her eyes
fixed on Nick's face while her brain struggled to process
this. Patric must have waited by the exit for them, she
realised with a chill of foreboding.

Tension stretched to breaking point. Determined to put
an end to it, she flashed a smile in Patric's direction and
improvised recklessly, 'It's time we moved on. Nice to see
you again, Patric. I hope your business here goes well for
you. Say goodbye, Nick.'

After a mildly exasperated glance—he was rather proud
of remembering his manners—Nick said politely, 'Goodbye, Mr Sutherland. Thank you for the drink.'

'Do you have a car?' Patric asked.

She knew what was coming. 'No, but we like riding on
the bus, don't we, Nick?'

'I'm sure Nick will enjoy my car.' Although Patric
spoke smoothly he didn't try to hide the mockery in his
eyes.

Reining in the irritation that would have revealed far too
much, she said, 'Oh, we can't take you out of your way.
The bus will be fine.'

'The bus will be hot and full.' His smile was subtly taunting. 'Whereas the car's in the parking building just around the corner.'

It wasn't like Patric to over-persuade. He'd never had to—people always fell in with his wishes. So why was he forcing the issue when he knew damned well that she didn't want anything more to do with him?

Nick looked from one to the other, his brows creasing slightly. 'Why can't we go with Mr Sutherland, Mummy?'

Desperation forced Kate's brain into swift, fruitful action. Collectedly she said, 'Of course we can. Thank you, it's very kind of you.'

Patric's eyes glinted with unholy appreciation of her capitulation. 'Let's go, then.'

The car was parked in the hotel basement. Large and dark green, it sat in an area ringed with notices warning people that this was a private car park.

'Cool,' Nick breathed. 'It's a Rolls Royce!' One of his intense, short-lived passions had been cars. 'Is it yours, Mr Sutherland?'

Patric opened the rear door for him. 'No, a friend lent it to me.'

Nick settled in the back and began to examine the fittings. As Patric closed the door on Kate in the front, she turned anxiously. 'Don't touch anything.'

'Not even the seat?'

'Don't you be smart with me, mister.' His grin soothed some tightly wound fear. Kate grinned back. 'Nothing else, all right?'

Patric opened the driver's door and slid behind the wheel. Kate's throat tightened. Too close—even in this huge car he was too close.

'Mummy,' Nick exclaimed, 'there's a television here!'

Kate forced a laugh. 'I'm not surprised—you could just about live in a car this size,' she said, holding her hands still in her lap.

Sitting in a vehicle was infinitely more intimate than

being across a table in a crowded café. Kate's heartbeat picked up speed. She concentrated on relaxing her taut muscles, and as the big car eased out of the parking bay she managed to say steadily, 'It's glorious weather, isn't it? I believe it's still raining at home.'

'New Zealand's having its wettest spring for decades,' Patric said.

His hands rested confidently on the wheel, long-fingered, competent—hands that could be tender, or excitingly fierce against a woman's soft skin…

The car drew up at an intersection. 'Where are you staying?' Patric asked, waiting on the lights.

'Robinson's Hotel is just this side of Cavill Avenue,' she said colourlessly.

'I know it.' He manoeuvred between two other cars, one driven by a tourist if its erratic progress was anything to judge by. 'It's a pleasant place, I believe,' he observed.

Kate's fingers clenched, loosened. 'Very pleasant.'

'How long have you been here?'

Her voice dropped. She hated lying. 'Since yesterday. I hope the weather stays like this, although Nick loved the thunderstorm we had this afternoon.'

'When storms start coming across the Gold Coast you know summer's on its way,' Patric said laconically. 'I'd like to see you again, Kate. And the boy.'

She'd been expecting some such request, bracing herself for it. Above the thick roar in her ears she heard her voice—cool, composed—say, 'I don't think that would be a good idea.'

'We have a lot to talk about.'

'We have nothing to talk about.' Denying the wild thunder of her pulses, she stared straight ahead.

'You could start by explaining why you didn't tell me almost seven years ago that you were pregnant,' he said, his deep, quiet voice edged with menace as he eased the huge car between the palms on either side of the entrance to Robinson's Hotel.

When a uniformed porter emerged, Nick pushed open the door and hopped out, looking around him with interest. Watching him carefully, Kate said huskily, 'It wouldn't have made much difference, Patric. I said then that I didn't want to continue our relationship. I'm saying it again. We have nothing in common—we never did.'

In the small, taut cocoon of silence that enclosed the front of the car, Patric said levelly, 'One of the things I always found so fascinating about you was the contrast between your intelligence and that doe-eyed, vulnerable face. I'll ring you.' Ruthlessness hardened his voice. 'My son won't grow up not knowing his father.'

White-lipped, Kate returned, 'It's not that simple, I'm afraid.' She had to force herself to continue, and all pretence of composure vanished as the short, ugly syllables dragged across her tongue. 'He's not your son.'

His long, well-cut mouth thinned into a cruel line. 'Don't lie, Kate.'

She shook her head. 'It's the truth.'

Quietly, lethally, he said, 'He was born almost exactly nine months after we made love.'

I can't bear this, she thought, pushing a shaking hand through the heavy mass of silken hair that clung to her neck and temples. But it had to be endured. In a hoarse voice she said, 'Nine months and two weeks.'

'I'm sure that's within the normal range of gestation,' he said curtly. 'You were a virgin. I remember it vividly.'

Kate opened her mouth, but he continued with icy detachment, 'And don't try telling me Nick's the son of your lover at university—you hadn't even gone to Christchurch when the boy would have been conceived.' Eyes hooded and dangerous, he added coldly, 'Besides, there was no lover.'

How did he know that?

He looked past her as Nick came up to her door. In an almost soundless voice Patric said, 'Try not to work yourself up. Nothing worthwhile is ever easy, but obstacles are made to be overcome. I'll ring you tomorrow morning. Don't make any plans for the day.'

She scrambled out. 'Goodbye, Patric,' she said unevenly, and took Nick's hand, leading him away from the Rolls towards the reception area of the apartment block.

Behind them, the car door closed with a soft, opulent thunk. Kate had to strain her ears to hear the vehicle whisper away. She didn't turn, didn't look back.

'Mummy,' Nick said, wide-eyed, 'why did we come here?'

'Oh, I just thought it might be fun to eat at the restaurant one day. Let's go and have a look at it, shall we?'

After a tour of the restaurant, and a discussion about the menu cards, they walked back into the vestibule. Kate couldn't prevent a swift glance through the large glass doors but of course the Rolls was long gone, its place taken by two taxis. 'When we get back home I want something cold to drink,' she said brightly. 'How about you?'

'A milkshake?'

'Why not?' She smiled at the porter as she and Nick went out through a side door and walked steadily beneath the palms that were the Gold Coast's signature plant, beside a wall brightened by a scarlet drape of bougainvillea, through beautifully manicured gardens.

A skateboarder shot past, slowing and stopping as they passed the entrance to a complex of pools. About fifteen, he grinned at them before stooping to adjust something on his skateboard. Kate and Nick went sedately past the tennis courts, eventually leaving the grounds through a small gate that opened onto the street behind.

'Mummy, *look*! There's a bungee jump!'

'No,' Kate said automatically. 'You're too young.'

He laughed, but stared longingly while they walked past the apparatus. His adolescence, Kate thought grimly, was going to be a nightmare, unless he found some pursuit that would safely satisfy his thirst for adventure.

Perhaps she could convince him that skateboarding was

the way to go, she thought as the noise of the boarder's wheels started up behind them again.

Reaction was setting in. Fear tasted coppery in her mouth and sweat trickled down her back. Sometimes she'd imagined meeting Patric again, but in her dreams it had been vastly different from that unnerving, violently painful experience.

Of course he assumed that he was Nick's father, but that was his problem, not hers. And when he thought it over, he'd realise she had no reason to lie. Then he'd go, and she and Nick would be safe again.

'What's the matter?' Nick asked, surprising her with his perception.

Fighting back apprehension and anger and self-pity, and a relentless, corroding grief, she said easily, 'I think I might be getting a headache.'

He looked guilty. 'Was it because you went on the roller-coaster?'

Kate laughed. 'No, darling, it wasn't. It's my stomach I have to watch out for on roller-coasters, not my head.'

'I don't,' he said smugly. He turned and watched the skateboarder surge out onto the footpath, then said in his most comforting voice, 'Never mind, we can go for a swim when we get back home and then your headache will go away.' After gazing at a vivid yellow mini-moke chugging along the road, its cargo of girls waving at every passer-by, he added thoughtfully, 'I don't s'pose Mr Sutherland has to worry about his stomach when he goes on roller-coasters.'

Kate had once watched Patric walk surely and swiftly across a narrow plank suspension bridge high above a gorge, not bothering to touch the single wire that others had clung to all the way across. He hadn't been showing off; he'd been in a hurry to get to her.

Ruthlessly suppressing the image, she said, 'I don't suppose so.'

She stepped to one side to let the skateboarder past, but

he seemed content to idle along behind them. Probably
eyeing the bungee jump too. What was it with some people
that made them want to terrify the wits out of themselves?
Adrenalin addiction?

Nick said, 'I didn't know Mr Sutherland came to Poto
when you were there. You didn't tell me about him, only
about Uncle Toby and Aunt Jean and your cousins all beginning with J—Juliet and Josephine and Jenny. And the
horses, and the swimming pool in the creek. Why haven't
I got cousins?'

It made her heart raw to talk about those days so long
ago, days perpetually hazed with summer's golden light.
'Because I didn't have any brothers and sisters.'

'I've got second cousins, though. How old were you
when your mummy and daddy were killed on Mount
Everest and you had to go and live with Aunt Jean and
Uncle Toby and the cousins?'

'Three.'

'Younger than me,' he said. They walked on in silence
until he asked casually, 'Did Mr Sutherland know *my* father?'

She'd told him his father was dead. It had weighed
heavily on her conscience, but she could think of no other
way to protect him from inevitable disillusion. Now, looking back on the lies she'd told Patric half an hour previously, she thought with a defeated irony that she was getting quite good at them.

Still, she'd lie her soul into hell for her son.

Aloud she said, 'The Poto Valley is a small place. He
might have.'

To her great relief Nick forgot about the past in the
excitement of pointing out a Harley motorcycle, all black
and shiny and reeking of machismo—unlike its small,
blonde, bikini-clad rider, her fine-featured face incongru-
ous beneath the helmet.

Kate didn't delude herself that Nick had said all he had
to say about Patric, but apparently he was satisfied for the

moment. As they turned down the road that led to their low-rise block of apartments she could feel the pressure lift, roll from her shoulders, easing stressed tendons and muscles. Now that they had escaped Patric that simmering anxiety would soon fade.

Late that night she realised that she'd been too optimistic. Restlessness and a chilly breath of foreboding drove her to put her book down, turn off the light and slide back the door onto the balcony. Leaning against the balustrade, she stared down at the courtyard, screened from it by fronds of the ever-present palms.

Although the air was warm, a heavy stillness probably indicated a towering thunderhead somewhere close by, ready to progress regally over the Gold Coast with maximum noise and drama; the property manager had told Nick that each summer they built up inland and moved down the escarpment, across the coastal plain and out to sea.

Someone had barbecued their dinner in the courtyard; the scent of sausages and steak and seafood hung on the air. Voices, punctuated by bursts of laughter, counterpointed the hum of traffic through this favoured strip of land with its long, beautiful beaches and glamorous tourist trade.

She'd been so happy when she'd won the prize, and she and Nick had had such fun planning the trip, such fun when she finally got here. What wilful, unkind fate had brought Patric to that hotel in time to see her on a rollercoaster?

And why hadn't almost seven years given her some defences against him?

Only two hours previously, when she'd showered before bed, she'd found herself staring at her brightly lit image. The mirrors at home were so small it was years since she'd seen herself full length.

Would Patric notice the changes? Her breasts were fuller—though still not voluptuous—and the flat plane of her stomach had rounded a little. Pregnancy had added slight stretchmarks on the soft gold of her skin—faded now to thin silver lines. Would he find them ugly?

No, she'd thought, furious with herself as she'd turned away, because he wasn't ever going to see them, or get the opportunity to realise anew how long her legs were. Or that the small amount of weight she'd lost had fined her down.

Now she stared blindly into the warm, seductive night, and reiterated that she couldn't afford to surrender to the weakness that drew her to him. Although she still found Patric wildly attractive, that wasn't important. His arrival in their lives threatened Nick's safety and well-being. That afternoon she'd had to run away.

What if Patric found them again?

How could he? Thousands of tourists inhabited the apartment blocks and hotels that lined the beach.

Rapidly, frowning into the night, she went over their conversation. No, he didn't know which theme parks they hadn't yet visited. Perhaps she should start thinking of an excuse not to go to any more. Nick would be angry and upset, but that would be infinitely safer than having Patric hunt them down.

Kate drew in a deep, ragged breath and realised that her fingers were clinging to the balustrade. Stepping back, she straightened her shoulders.

Should they just go home?

No, that was overreacting. Patric was here on business; he'd have neither the time nor the ability to stand outside every theme park looking for her and Nick. Her mouth tilted in a humourless smile as she imagined him split into several Patrics, each hard and confident and authoritative, waiting impatiently outside every park. All they had to do was stay away and he'd never find them.

Patric might watch the airport at Brisbane, but they only had four days to go instead of the week she'd intimated, so they should be out of Australia and home in New Zealand before he posted anyone there.

And once they were back in New Zealand he'd never find them. New Zealand phone books were filled with K. Browns, so even if he looked in the Whangarei book he wouldn't recognise her.

Anyway, why would he think of Whangarei, a small provincial city, two hours' drive north of Auckland and more than five hours away from Poto?

Her mouth trembled. It was so unfair; she'd done nothing wrong, yet she was forced to hide.

Still, it was for Nick. And for Nick she would do anything. He was all she lived for, the only thing that made her life worthwhile.

The next day Kate organised a trip to a bird sanctuary where—to Nick's stunned delight—hundreds of brilliantly coloured lorikeets, luminously blue and red and gold, swished in to feed from trays of specially prepared food held high by hopeful tourists.

Kate took photographs of her son's absorbed, fascinated face as two, then four birds rocketed down and landed on his tray, squabbling and noisy as only parrots can be, scrambling to eat the sticky preparation. Another swooped low and landed on his shoulder, complaining vociferously as it tried to get at the syrup.

Carefully, his face oddly white beneath his cap, Nick held the tray aloft in clenched hands.

Quarrelling and pushing, the birds ate greedily until some unknown alarm signal sent them whirling and wheeling upwards in a ragged, pulsating spiral that streamed across the tops of the trees and out of sight.

'Mummy!' Nick breathed. Unable for once to speak, he gazed up at her, and then his face changed and he said, 'Hello, Mr Sutherland, did you see the birds? Did you see them on me? Did you see the one on my shoulder? I could feel its claws in my skin!'

CHAPTER TWO

IN THE past Kate had been threatened with death, she'd endured agony and degradation and sheer horror, but she had never known such a blast of fear as she knew then. Nick's face swung dizzily; thank God he wasn't looking at her.

Forcing her shocked features into immobility, she realised she was pressing a clenched fist to her heart, trying to contain its tumult. She dragged a breath into her labouring lungs. This was no coincidence; how could she have thought she'd escaped him?

'Hello, Patric,' she said, and was dimly proud of her steady voice.

His smile had a predatory edge. 'Hello, Kate. Yes, I saw the bird,' he told Nick. 'What did its claws feel like?'

'Little and scratchy,' Nick said, 'but it held on tight.' He beamed. 'Lots of people took my photo, and so did Mummy. I can show the class at school. And we went all around this park and saw koala bears and wombats, and birds in a high, high place like a cage.'

'An aviary,' Kate said thinly.

'Would you like something to eat and drink now that the lorikeets have gone? I know a place with a pool where birds come up to the verandah.' Patric looked down at Nick with a smile that held nothing of the hidden antagonism he'd directed at Kate.

Nick said politely, 'Yes, thank you.'

By the time Kate had got herself together it was too late; they were walking across the open space towards the gate—just like a family, some soggily sentimental part of her thought wistfully. She could protest, but it would only put off the inevitable reckoning. Better to face him.

'How did you get here?' Patric asked as they walked out of the sanctuary.

'We came in a bus,' Nick said helpfully. 'We've got a car at home, though—a Mini called Eugene.'

'I'll take you back to your apartment after we've had something to eat,' Patric said, without looking at Kate, although his steely tone was directed at her.

Nick grinned at him. 'In the Rolls Royce?' he asked.

'Not this time.' Patric's dark gaze rested on the boy's face with something like hunger.

Kate flinched; so he hadn't believed her. Now she'd have to explain exactly what had happened, and although she'd recovered from the trauma the sordid experience still sickened her. Apart from the therapist who'd helped her deal with it she'd told no one, and if asked to choose the last person in the world she'd want to reveal the truth to, she'd have picked Patric.

But she couldn't let him go on thinking that Nick was his son. And after she'd convinced him, she'd have to swear him to secrecy.

Ignoring her completely, he said, 'No, not a Rolls Royce today. My friend needed it to take his dog to the vet.'

The replacement was, however, large and opulent; judging by Nick's open appreciation, it too was something special in the car line.

Silently Kate allowed herself to be put into the front seat. Since that first icy blast of antagonism Patric hadn't looked at her. How the hell had he found them? She'd thought she'd been so clever, but he'd been even cleverer.

That was Patric—always one step ahead. At eighteen, and as green as grass, Kate had been impressed by his brilliance. Oh, she wasn't stupid, and she'd done very well at school, but everyone knew that Patric had a formidable brain.

As well as wealth, six glamorous, experienced years had

separated the son and heir to the Sutherland aviation empire from the niece of his parents' farm manager. Well and
truly out of her depth, the young Kate had been awed by
invitations to the homestead, moonstruck by the heady excitement of being the woman Patric wanted. Yet although
the summer holidays had passed in a whirl of activity
amongst the friends and visitors who flocked every year to
Tatamoa, she'd been alone, lost in love.

Ignoring her aunt, who'd warned Kate that no good
would come of her pursuit, as she saw it, of their em-
ployer's son—even taking no notice of kind, regal Mrs
Sutherland, who had told her gently but decisively that
Patric was not for her—she had danced on to an inevitable
reckoning, registering nothing but her feverish, reckless
dreams.

How dazed she had been when Patric told her he loved
her—those three words that wove a snare about her, the
delusion that dazzled and enchanted her into his bed. She'd
so desperately wanted it to be true that she'd let herself
believe it. It had been the sum of all her hopes, and she'd
thought that nothing could ever go wrong again.

How young she'd been!

She turned to check that Nick was belted in, and for a
moment met Patric's eyes, so cold they froze her heart.

No sign of love there now, she thought cynically. She
didn't belong in Patric's high-flying, moneyed world, but
then he didn't belong in hers either.

He took them to a pleasant, cool restaurant beside a park
where water splashed over rocks into a small lakelet.
Beneath the dark, feathery foliage of sheoak trees sedate
ibises lifted black, bare heads and begged for food, their
white bodies making them look like a sinister *corps de
ballet*.

'Don't give them anything,' Patric directed Nick as the
waitress showed them out onto a wide screened verandah.
'They don't need it and they can become a nuisance.'

'Like the sparrows and seagulls at home.' Nick nodded,

watching the birds with interest. 'I s'pose that's why there aren't many seagulls here—the ibises take all the food. Why do you think the birds here sing in the daytime and they don't at home?'

Kate, who'd already tried to deal with this, was impressed when Patric said briskly, 'I have no idea, but you should be able to find out. Are you interested in birds?'

Nick looked puzzled. 'I just want to know,' he said.

'The story of your life,' Kate told him drily, adding without emphasis, 'Nick has a driving curiosity.'

Patric lifted his brows slightly. The powerful face was unreadable, as were his eyes. He said with questionable pleasantness, 'It shows he's got an active mind,' before switching his attention back to Nick. 'What would you like to eat?'

Nick chose a sandwich and a milkshake.

Black brows raised, Patric looked at Kate.

'Coffee, thank you,' she said. Normally she drank tea, but an extra charge of caffeine would be welcome. A faint queasiness persuaded her to add, 'And I'll have a sandwich too.'

'Club?' he asked.

Shock silenced her for long enough to cause an awkward pause. He'd remembered her juvenile addiction to club sandwiches, she thought, almost dizzy with a suspect pleasure. Or was he trying to reinforce her memory of that long-ago summer when he'd wooed her and won her? To cover her confusion she gazed at the menu. 'I haven't had a club sandwich for years,' she said composedly, 'but it sounds lovely.'

He ordered, and asked for a jug of iced water. When it arrived Nick downed half a glass with gusto and chattered on, asking questions and answering the ones addressed to him with open ingenuousness.

Kate sat stiffly, ready to intervene if Patric should want to know things she needed to keep hidden. However, he didn't step over her unspoken boundaries, and gradually she relaxed back into the chair.

She'd forgotten his intense, crackling vitality; not purely sexual, it gave life to those enigmatic, unsettling eyes, modified the control he exerted over his features and humanised the dominant, uncompromising framework of his face. Although his mouth was beautifully moulded no one would ever call him a conventionally handsome man, yet even when he'd been barely twenty people had swivelled as he'd walked into a room, drawn by his charismatic, disturbing masculinity.

Now, Kate thought wearily, he took her breath away. Time and authority had reinforced that enviable assurance, and the whole magnetic male package was buttressed by a sexual glitter all the more compelling for being so firmly leashed. Part of it was the contrast between the colouring he'd inherited from his Spanish mother—bronze skin, black hair, and eyes of cold, dark grey—and the austere bone structure and build that had been handed down through his Scottish ancestors.

Perhaps, she thought cynically, part of that attraction was the armour of money and position.

The aviation empire left to Patric by Alex Sutherland, his father, had been founded by his grandfather, 'Black' Pat, on Tatamoa station airstrip and every summer Alex, Pilar and Patric—always accompanied by Alex's widowed sister Barbara Cusack and her son Sean, and usually by other family and friends—had spent the Christmas holidays on Tatamoa, arriving with all the drama and panache of exotic migrating birds. For the month they'd been in residence the Poto Valley had buzzed, only settling down to a quieter, more mundane life once they'd departed.

Kate took a sip of water and allowed her attention to wander as Patric and Nick began to discuss snakes. It amused her that from other tables on the big verandah other women glanced covertly at Patric. Join the throng, she thought, so caught up in her recollections that Patric's question barely impinged, and by the time she registered what he'd asked it was too late.

'In Whangarei,' Nick was saying chattily. 'In Stanner Street. I go to Whau Valley School and Mum works in a dress shop in Cameron Street. She only goes until I come home from school, but sometimes she has to work late and then I stay with Mr and Mrs Schumaker next door, or my friend Rangi MacArthur just down the road. I'm in J2, and I can read the best—'

He wasn't boasting, but Kate interrupted sharply, 'That's enough, Nick.' Too late, she thought with sick dismay. Oh, why hadn't she kept her wits about her?

Because she couldn't control a stupid, unwarranted jealousy!

Nick said reasonably, 'Mummy, you know I can—'

'I know.' Switching her gaze to Patric, she said in a voice that made her son stare at her, 'Ask *me* any questions you want answered.'

'I don't know that I'd trust you to be as veracious as Nick,' he said, leaning back in his seat and surveying her with an oblique smile. 'Why did you move to Whangarei?'

The damage was done now. Stiffly Kate said, 'I needed a place to live.'

'Why didn't you stay with your aunt and uncle?'

She looked out over the lake. 'Nick, look! There's a black swan.' Waiting until he was absorbed in the sight, she went on remotely, 'You probably don't remember, but they left Tatamoa after I went back to university. It was exactly a week after the May holidays when you and I met for the last time. My cousins and I had all left home by then, so my aunt and uncle decided on a complete change of direction and went off to manage a motel in the Cook Islands.'

Nick transferred his absorbed attention from the swan to a woman who'd just been shown to a table. Tanned and slender, she flicked back long silver-gilt hair that dazzled above her white clothes. As she stared blankly out across the pool, ringed fingers tapped impatiently on the table. Gold chains festooned her tanned throat; more were looped around her thin wrists.

'You're staring,' Kate said in a low voice.

Nick's eyes switched from the woman to a family at the next table.

'Why didn't you go with them?' Patric asked.

'I didn't want to.' Shocked, humiliated, deeply disturbed and feeling like trash—incapable of behaving rationally— she'd been unable to tell them she was pregnant.

'You dropped out of university,' he said. 'Where did you go then?'

Astonished, she looked at him, meeting eyes as disinterested and purposeful as weapons. 'How do you know?'

'I got someone to check.' He smiled at her, showing his teeth. 'The same man who discovered that you'd lied in May, when you flung your new lover in my teeth.'

Kate cast a harried glance at Nick, but he was exchanging tentative smiles with a girl his own age at the next table.

'You stopped going to lectures in June, and disappeared.' Patric paused before finishing, 'When I discovered that, I rang your aunt and uncle, only to discover they were no longer at Tatamoa. I was told they'd gone to Australia. I assumed you'd gone with them—and that you didn't contact me because you didn't want to.' His eyes left her, settled on Nick's face. 'You should have come to me,' he said evenly.

'I didn't need to. I managed.' Her voice was distant as she forced memories back into the bitter past, refusing to let their bleakness stain the present. She even managed to keep her tone steady as she added, 'You had no connection with the—the situation I found myself in.'

'I'd have helped, Kate.' His voice roughened, sending a shiver the length of her spine. 'Why didn't you tell me?'

Tempted to ask what his brand-new wife would have thought if Kate had turned up pregnant, she bit the words back. That would be indicating he might have some claim to Nick. 'It had nothing to do with you,' she repeated.

He scrutinised her with dark impenetrable eyes. 'I despise liars,' he said levelly.

Kate drew in a deep breath, deliberately relaxing the tense muscles in her face and neck. 'That must make you feel immensely superior.'

A pulse flicked in his jaw. Glancing again at Nick to make sure he still wasn't paying attention, Kate added stubbornly, 'It's not important now, anyway. It was a long time ago and things have changed completely.'

Far from listening to them, Nick was staring with appalled fascination at one of the children in the nearby family party, a small, black-eyed blonde of three or so who'd begun a spectacular tantrum.

Patric said softly, 'You can never be free of the past, Kate, never. It casts a long shadow.'

Before she could react to what had sounded like a direct threat his smile banished her pain and her fear, and for a few seconds she was young, silly Kate Brown again, all eyes and hair and worshipful wonder, dazzled and overawed and lost in the depthless, dangerous seas of first love.

Fortunately the arrival of their orders gave her the chance to huddle into the tatters of her self-control.

'That waitress liked you, Mr Sutherland,' Nick observed when they were alone again. 'She kept looking at you.'

'I liked her too,' Patric said. 'Can you manage that big sandwich?'

'I'm hungry,' he said with gusto, eyeing his plate with every appearance of satisfaction. 'Her hair was red on the ends and black by her head.'

'She dyes it,' Kate told him.

'You don't dye your hair, do you?'

'Your mother's hair has always been that colour,' Patric said, his glance lingering on the thick, glossy tresses. 'She used to wear it longer, though.'

'When she was a little girl?'

'She was fourteen when her uncle came to work for my father,' Patrick said easily.

'When I'm fourteen I'll be grown up and I can look after you,' Nick told his mother.

'That's a lovely thought, but I'll probably be old enough to look after myself by then. You'd better start on that food, or we might have to go before you've finished.'

The thought of leaving it behind filled him with such horror that he settled into silently dismembering it.

'Excuse me?'

The strident voice with its upward intonation startled them all—except Patric, Kate noticed. He got to his feet as the woman with the silver-gilt hair arrived at their table, gold chains gleaming expensively. Nick stared at Patric, then scrambled to his feet too, wringing Kate's heart.

Ignoring Kate and Nick, the woman flashed a practised smile at Patric. 'You don't happen to have a light, do you? I seem to have lost mine.'

'No, I'm sorry,' he said, and turned his head towards the serving station. Immediately the waitress headed towards them. Patric waited until she'd got there, then asked her for matches.

The silver-gilt woman treated him to a lingering smile, thanked him, and went back to her table.

Nick eyed her thoughtfully as he sat down. '*She* liked you too,' he said. 'She's pretty. But not as pretty as you, Mummy—is she, Mr Sutherland?'

Patric took the opportunity to scrutinise Kate's face. Although his hard-edged face showed no emotion, she saw a dark glint in the depths as he said gravely, 'Nowhere near as pretty.'

Heat flared across Kate's skin. Lightly, with a meaningless smile, she returned, 'Thank you. You're remarkably handsome too.'

'Not pretty.' Horrified, Nick emphasised both words.

Unexpectedly, Kate and Patric laughed together. 'No,' Kate reassured him, 'Not at all pretty.'

For a moment she and Patric hovered on the brink of some sort of harmony, a fragile rapport that shattered when he said, 'You have a babysitting service at your apartments, I understand?'

'I believe so,' Kate replied guardedly, forestalling him by adding, 'But I have no intention of using it.'

'I'd like to see you tonight,' he said, his face as purposeful as his voice. 'Nick—'

She overrode him. 'That wouldn't be a good idea,' she said. 'Eat up, Nick.'

'Kate,' Patric said, the iron determination beneath the words sending a shiver down her spine, 'we need to talk.'

Her brain was as useless as cotton wool. Patric had no claims on either her or Nick—worse, he might well reveal her whereabouts to the one man she feared and loathed—yet she had to stiffen every muscle in her body before she could say, 'No.'

He leaned back and surveyed her, his cold eyes implacable, the stark bone structure of his face giving him an impressive force and power. 'Yes,' he contradicted. 'Don't you like your sandwich?'

She pushed the plate a little to one side, picking up her cup with a shaking hand. 'I'm not hungry,' she said, hoping the coffee would banish the slow shudders that started somewhere in her heart and were spreading through her in wintry waves.

'I'm not surprised,' he said, mockery flicking each word. 'I'd have found out eventually, Kate. New Zealand's too small for secrets to lie hidden for ever.'

This secret would, she thought grimly, even if she and Nick had to leave Whangarei, stealing away like refugees. She drank the coffee, barely tasting it; strong, hot, and laden with caffeine, it still didn't warm her.

Nothing could, she thought into the lengthening silence—not the sun, not the light that licked across Nick's dark head as he solidly masticated his way through his food.

Patric wouldn't give up. He thought Nick was his son, and he was determined to play some part in the boy's life. But once he knew the truth he wouldn't care. So she'd have to tell him the truth—or as much of it as she could tailor to this situation. And then she'd have to swear him to silence.

'I know what you're thinking,' she said bleakly, 'but it isn't so.'

His eyes branded her a liar. 'If I'd known—'

'It doesn't matter,' she said desperately. 'There's no reason for you to think that anything was your responsibility. None at all.'

He said with cool, searing irony, 'Nice try, Kate. We'll discuss this later.'

Although her nerves felt like slowly shredding tissue paper, she said, 'Nick, look, there's a pukeko.'

He swung around. 'Pukekos are a New Zealand bird,' he said after a long, considering stare.

Patric said, 'Yes, but they're also quite common here.'

Nick's brows drew into a knot. 'So how did they get here from New Zealand?' he asked. 'Or from New Zealand to here?'

Patric's mouth twisted. 'The winds usually blow from Australia to New Zealand, so I imagine that thousands of years ago a couple of very tough pukekos—one male, one female—were lifted by cyclonic winds in Australia and carried all the way across the Tasman Sea, to land in New Zealand with a huge sigh of relief.'

Nick grinned. 'Birds don't sigh. I bet they were happy, though, when they got there.'

Patric asked Kate quietly, brusquely, 'Are you all right?'

'Yes.'

'Would you like some more coffee?'

'No, thank you.' So much, she thought sickly, for caffeine as a stimulant. She poured a glass of water and drank it down while Nick finished his sandwich.

'Time to go,' she said, hoping her voice sounded cool

and casual. Although it wouldn't fool Patric, she didn't
want her son worried.

'OK,' he said cheerfully, but as they left the restaurant
he took her hand, an unusual enough event for her to vow
that nothing—especially not Patric Sutherland—would be
allowed to upset him.

In the car Patric asked, 'Back to your apartment?'

'Yes, thank you,' she said rigidly. 'How did you know
where we're staying?'

For a moment she didn't think he was going to tell her.
Then he said, 'You don't lie well, even by omission. I paid
a passing skateboarder to follow you.'

So the young man with a blond ponytail who'd trailed
her and Nick from Robinson's Hotel to their apartment
building had been Patric's spy. Clever. And typical.

Although the traffic had thickened, Patric guided the car
through it with skill and courtesy. He did everything
well—danced superbly, played sport skilfully, and made
love with such heart-shattering brilliance that the effects
still lingered after all these years.

It was just as well she'd grown past that juvenile infat-
uation, Kate thought savagely. Otherwise she could be in
real danger.

As the car drew to a halt she said with an enormous,
bitter reluctance, 'I'll see you tomorrow night.'

He put on the handbrake. 'Tomorrow night—yes, all
right. We'll go out to dinner. I'll call for you at seven.'

Already regretting her decision, she gave a stiff nod. It
had to be done, even if telling him was going to tear her
apart. But it wouldn't do that; she was much stronger than
she'd been when she was eighteen.

And going to a restaurant would give them the buffer
of other people, of the need to act in a civilised manner.

Patric said silkily, 'Just don't go thinking you can slip
off to New Zealand tomorrow. I know enough about you
now to track you down.'

Well, perhaps she deserved that. 'Say thank you to Mr Sutherland,' she told Nick.

He made his thanks, and when the car drew away said eagerly, 'Can I go with you tomorrow night?'

'No, darling.'

He was ready to object, but she said, 'Come on, we've got time for a swim before dinner,' and he forgot about it.

He'd remember later, but by then she'd have recovered a bit of her normal spirit. At the moment she was too exhausted to deal with her son in a stubborn mood.

That night she twisted sleeplessly in her bed, trying to work out some sort of strategy for the meeting.

Fate, she thought grimly, was a bitch. Why did Patric have to be at that hotel when she and Nick were on the roller-coaster? Everything had been going so well—she'd achieved a measure of serenity and centred a quietly satisfying life around her son and her work. If occasionally she thought wistfully of the hopes and dreams that single motherhood had put paid to, Nick made up for everything.

If only she'd managed to see Patric first!

Restlessness clawed at her, hummed with reckless intensity through her body. Eventually she got up and walked across to the window. Although it was well after midnight cars still purred along the roads, and lights in the surrounding high-rise buildings showed that most of the Gold Coast was still awake. She looked up into the sky.

Once Patric had told her the names of the stars, pointing out the constellations—Orion the summer hunter, riding high with Sirius at heel, the fuzzy glow of the Pleiades, the wheeling cross of the south. She'd been intrigued, so the next time they met he'd brought a pair of binoculars and shown her the coloured stars in the Jewel Box and the red glitter of Antares, and they'd discussed the likelihood of life on planets around those distant stars.

She found to her surprise that she was crying, noiseless sobs that ached in her throat. How stupid—she hadn't cried for years! Stiffening her shoulders, she blew her nose and wiped her eyes; she'd been so young, so silly, a naïve country kid from the backblocks, and she'd had to grow up in such a hurry.

Sex and pregnancy had a habit of doing that to you, she thought cynically. Very maturing.

Even though each of the years between her eighteen and his twenty-four might have been a century, she'd loved Patric with all the ardour of her young, untried heart. Fascinated throughout her teens by his dark aura, she'd always watched him shyly from a distance, but the year she'd turned sixteen she'd fallen in love as only the young can—headlong and wholly—and to her delight and surprise he'd smiled at her with narrowed, gleaming eyes.

That had been the beginning.

Those holidays he'd introduced her to kisses—gentle, tender kisses, making due allowance for her innocence, apparently unaware that beneath the pressure of his already experienced mouth she'd melted, burned, flamed into incandescence.

Or perhaps he had known, she thought now, staring down at the shifting, fractured lights through the palms. He'd made sure they were almost never alone; when they rode the station horses, when he'd taught her to water-ski on the dam, when he'd played tennis with her, other people had acted as buffers.

Yes, he'd probably been well aware of her ardent, untutored response. He'd been careful and kind—and cruel, because even then she'd known there could be no future for them. That year her aunt, worried by this unusual friendship, had told her not to get her hopes up, that Patric would eventually marry a girl from his own circle. Someone like Laura Williams, the daughter of his father's best friend.

Kate's mouth clamped into a hard, tight line.

After those holidays Patric had left for America, where he'd been doing a graduate degree in some form of business studies, and she'd grieved for a lost dream.

The first postcard had filled her with excitement and relief, and although he never wrote much more than a sentence or two, and the cards arrived infrequently, they'd kept alive a spark of hope.

The following year he'd come back for a week; their meetings had been short, but he'd kissed her with much less restraint, and she'd learned just how intense sensual excitement could be.

Then at the end of her last year at school he'd finally returned, infinitely more sophisticated after two years abroad, and set in motion the turbulent trail of events that had led them to tomorrow's meeting—and indirectly to the boy who slept so peacefully in the next room.

The babysitter turned out to be a pleasant middle-aged woman who got on with Nick immediately. She said they'd swim, they'd watch a video, and after that he'd go to bed.

Grinning, Nick teased, 'At ten o'clock.'

'At eight o'clock,' Kate said firmly.

The babysitter laughed. 'Don't worry, eight o'clock it'll be.'

Since they'd arrived home from yet another theme park, Nick had prowled around the unit, demanding more attention than usual. He wasn't used to being left behind; their social life was the sort that included children. Now he asked, 'Where are you going, Mum?'

'I don't know,' she said, 'but when Mr Sutherland comes I'll get a phone number so that if I'm needed I can come straight back home. He'll probably have a mobile, but if he doesn't he can give me the number of the restaurant.'

He looked relieved. 'All right,' he said.

The intercom rang. Kate lifted the receiver and her heart jolted as Patric's voice said, 'Kate.'

'Can we have a telephone number?' she said. 'Just in case there's an emergency.'

After giving her a number, which she copied down, he said, 'I'll come up.'

'No,' she said. 'I'll be right down.'

She hung up and stooped to kiss Nick. His arms came around her a little fiercely. 'See you,' he said valiantly.

Straightening, she smiled at him. 'I won't be late, but I expect to find you sound asleep.'

It took all of Kate's determination to get herself to the comfortable, featureless foyer. And her stretched nerves were twisted into knots by the sight of Patric, tall and hard-edged and completely in control of himself and his world.

Although she no longer loved him, she was still strongly affected by his presence, by the blazing vitality that seared through his well-cut, informal clothes and proclaimed the alpha male.

Narrowed eyes—impersonal as the dark heart of thunderstorm—surveyed her. Kate's chin came up in the slightest gesture of defiance. No doubt he was accustomed to escorting women who wore designer clothes rather than a dress bought in the shop sale. However the soft gold echoed the colour of her skin and contrasted with her blue-green eyes.

'You take my breath away,' he said quietly.

Her heart jumped. 'Thank you,' she replied, the stilted words difficult on her tongue.

'I see very little difference from the girl I remember.'

Her hair swirled around her shoulders as she shook her head. 'Outwardly, perhaps.'

An old anguish ached through her like the phantom pain from an amputated limb; she had done her grieving for the Patric of Tatamoa. This man, tempered by unknown fires, a man of steel and disciplined aggression, was a different person: compelling, magnetic—much more dangerous.

'I hope you have changed,' he said, taking her arm to guide her to the car.

Sensation shivered through her in a mixture of flame and ice. 'Why?'

Once they were in motion he said, 'If you don't change you stagnate. I was a careless young fool with nothing but my own needs and desires in mind. You, of all people, should remember that. I'm not like that now.'

'I remember you being a leader—responsible and courageous and daring,' she said simply.

'Even when I made love to you and left you pregnant?' he asked with self-derisory contempt.

She glanced from her hands to his profile, an arrogant outline against the shimmering lights of the sea front. Screwing her courage to the sticking point, she said, 'You aren't Nick's father.'

His mouth tightened into a forbidding line. 'It won't work, Kate. I know his birth date—'

She interrupted jerkily, 'Patric, I tried to tell you before—you're not his father. Why would I lie to you?'

'I intend to find out.'

In any other situation she'd have been afraid of the menacing purr beneath the words. Now it merely reinforced her decision.

He put on the indicator and waited until they were halfway across the road before saying, 'So you slept with someone else within a week or so of making love to me.'

For a moment her mouth trembled. Controlling it, she said in a hard, flat voice, 'A fortnight later, to be exact.'

'Just after you went to Christchurch.'

She hesitated. 'Just before.'

He turned the wheel, and the car headed straight for a waterfall at the front of a small apartment block on the beach side of the road. Kate cried out, but beneath and to one side of the glittering curtain of water gaped an entrance, and this was where the car was heading.

'Where is this?' she asked huskily.

'My apartment. I certainly didn't want to discuss this in public. We'll eat there.'

'No!'

But the barred screen across the parking basement was already rumbling back.

'It's all right,' Patric said silkily as they drove down, 'You'll be perfectly safe while you tell me who else you slept with all those years ago, and how you know that Nick is his son and not mine.'

When the car had halted in a designated slot he switched off the engine. Into the silence he said with barely leashed antagonism, 'And why, when we met that last time in the May holidays, although you must have known you were pregnant, you didn't bother to tell me.'

CHAPTER THREE

HER swift glance at Patric's profile tightened every sinew in Kate. Ruthlessly she repressed the unjustified fear. She'd made the decision; she'd force down the crawling revulsion and tell him.

And then, she thought with a sudden stab of pain as he opened her door, the hope she'd never been able to stifle would be shown for what it was—hope's poor relation, wishful thinking. One act of violence almost seven years ago had shattered her dreams, made even friendship impossible between Patric and her.

Together they walked across the well-lit basement and took a lift to the penthouse. Naturally, Kate thought with a struggling sense of irony, trying to keep her mind away from the disclosures to come; of course Patric would be in the penthouse! Nothing but the best for the owner and managing director of Sutherland Aviation.

The lift doors opened onto a thickly carpeted hall. Without speaking, Patric unlocked a door and led her into the apartment.

A huge sitting room stretched out before her, decorated in the soft colours fashionable in south-eastern Queensland—a ceramic tiled floor half hidden by an off-white and blue Chinese rug, leather-covered sofas and chairs, a creamy amber travertine table surrounded by apricot dining chairs in a vaguely French style, and pictures on the walls selected for their inability to offend. It looked rich and cool and impersonal, all surface and no individuality.

If everything had been chosen to contrast forcefully with the dominant, uncompromising man who closed the door behind Kate, it couldn't have been done better. Masterful, disturbing on a primal level, Patric made the luxurious room dwindle and fade around him; even the splendid sweep of the ocean through the wall of glass doors took second place to his personality.

'Sit down.' He waited until she'd taken one of the leather chairs before asking with an unyielding courtesy that shivered across Kate's exposed nerves, 'Would you like a drink?'

'No, thank you,' she said quietly, stopping her fingers from worriedly smoothing the soft suede 'But you have something.'

'I think it would be a good idea if I abstained too,' he said, dark eyes watching—watching, weighing and measuring as they roamed her face.

'Look, let's get this over and done with.' Carefully controlling the desperation that roiled beneath each word, she said, 'Nick is not your son, Patric. Please believe me.'

'Why should I?'

'I'm telling you the truth. I ask you again—why would I lie?'

'Revenge?' His voice was expressionless.

She couldn't believe her ears. 'Why would I want revenge?'

'Because I married Laura six weeks after the last time we met and exactly four and half months after I'd sworn undying love for you.'

'No,' Kate said stonily. 'I told you at Tatamoa in the May holidays that it was over. You had every right to marry Laura.'

It was the truth, yet would she have been so adamant if she hadn't been kept informed of the other woman's presence in his life?

Lifting gritty eyelids, Kate looked directly at him. 'If there was any chance you might be Nick's father I'd have contacted you. But you're not.'

'Tell me about the man you slept with so soon after you

slept with me,' he suggested levelly, those hard eyes probing, his mouth twisted.

Kate closed her eyes for a second. But she'd lied to him, made him believe this, and she had to live with her lies. Raising her lashes, she shrugged. It took a lot of effort. Forcing her voice into an unnatural steadiness, she said, 'You said you knew there wasn't any man. Why did you send someone to Christchurch to pry into my affairs?'

Violence broke shockingly through the armour of his self-control as he swore. With a white line around his mouth he demanded, 'Why the hell do you think I did? I was in love with you—I went down to Tatamoa to ask you to marry me! When you told me so easily, so calmly, so definitely that it was over, all I could think of was that making love to you had scared you, or repelled you so much you couldn't bear to be in the same room as me.'

'No!'

His eyes narrowed. 'I told you I loved you, that I'd wait for you, the day after we'd made love. Remember? I rang because my father was dying—it was only a matter of time before his heart gave out, and I had to go back to Auckland to be with him.'

'I remember,' she said, her heart shaking. She'd been so sorry for him, and yet his hasty departure had dimmed her trembling, nascent joy. 'I understood,' she added.

'Did you understand that I was going to have to work eighteen hours every day to pull Sutherland's back into shape?'

She lifted her chin. 'I didn't know it was in trouble, but I certainly accepted that your place was with your parents.'

'That's why I didn't come down to see you during that first term. I couldn't leave my parents; my mother had collapsed, and my father deteriorated when I did go out of town,' he said, the decisive voice so lacking in emotion that it sounded pitiless as stone. 'And although you seemed distant when I rang, and your letters were the sort good little girls write to their cousins, I thought it was because you were so young, and because I couldn't be with you.'

Kate's hand went out towards him; she snatched it back as though it had touched an invisible flame, but he saw. 'Of course you had to stay with your father—and your mother. It wasn't that.'

He reined in his temper. 'Then what happened to make you change your mind? I know you loved me—you wouldn't have made love with me if you hadn't. Why didn't you tell me you were pregnant that day in the May holidays?'

'Because it was nothing to do with you. The baby wasn't—isn't—yours.' Nausea clutched her. 'Anyway, none of that matters now. All that's important is that Nick is not your son. Please believe me.'

She tried to keep any note of pleading from her voice but he must have heard it, because he gave her a glance in which anger and disgust were equally blended.

He hadn't sat down. Now he rested his hands on the back of one of the dining chairs and turned to look out over the white beach, glimmering in the swift-falling dusk. Against the wide purple sea his profile was an arrogant statement of strength. In an icily sardonic voice he asked, 'How can I? The Kate I knew, the Kate I fell in love with, wouldn't have slept with another man.'

Some frozen cinder in her heart, long dead, glowed softly. Ignoring it, she reiterated bleakly, 'I'm sorry. I wish he was, but Nick isn't yours, Patric.'

His face clamped into an expression of such fury that she had to stop herself from jumping to her feet and running. 'So whose is he?' he asked roughly.

'He's the son of the man who raped me a fortnight after you left Poto—a fortnight after your father's heart attack,' she said woodenly. 'A week after I'd had a period.' The words slid over her tongue like poisoned pebbles, bitter as rue, harsh with conviction.

For several taut, charged seconds he stared at her while

her pulse thundered in her ears. And then he swore, and she cried out with horror as he lifted the chair and crashed it onto the tiles.

She knew that she couldn't tell him the whole truth.

He looked at the maltreated chair as though it was abhorrent to him, then set it precisely back in place and strode silently across to the window, moving with the loose-limbed, deadly litheness of some big predatory animal. 'Who was he? The man who raped you?'

His voice was cold, so cold...

But beneath the cold control hid raw, uncaged savagery, a feral anger that lifted every hair on her skin. Only once before had she heard him speak in that tone—when Sean Cusack, his cousin, had tried to kiss her and fondle her.

She had no desire to hear it again.

'Nobody I knew,' she said quickly, already committed, speaking more easily now that she knew he believed her. 'He was hitch-hiking to Auckland. I was in the wrong place at the wrong time.' All lies—but her story was made more believable by the fact that the basis was true.

In that same lethal, almost soundless voice, Patric asked, 'What happened to him?'

'He stole a car from the Forsythes in Poto and smashed it into a bank fifty kilometres down the road. He died.' If Patric went looking for evidence that she was telling the truth, he'd find it written up in the newspapers of the time. Forgive me, she begged that dead thief.

Patric's dark brows drew together in a frown. 'Is that why you told me you were no longer in love with me? Because you were raped?'

Her hands gripped the glove-soft leather of the chair, then loosened. She folded them in her lap and kept them still by sheer determination. Steadily, without emphasis, she said, 'Yes. I was shattered—I couldn't bear the thought of any sort of intimacy. It's a common response.' She hesitated, then added, 'And I knew you were seeing a lot of Laura. In a way it seemed meant.'

Truth, she thought bitterly, has an infinite number of facets.

He turned to face her, the arrogant framework of his face very prominent. 'How did you know I was seeing Laura?'

'Do you remember my cousin Juliet? Your father gave her a job at Sutherland Aviation in Auckland.'

Older, more sophisticated and genuinely concerned, Juliet had tried to convince Kate that, sweet though a summer flirtation might be, it meant nothing. While Kate had been enduring a term of torment at university in Christchurch, her cousin's letters had been full of Patric. And Laura.

'I remember.' Patric's voice was distant.

His next question told her nothing, except that he was once more fully in control of himself. 'Did you go to the police?' he asked conversationally.

She bit her lip. 'It was my word against his. I didn't think anyone would believe me.' Sean had told her that. Sickened by his vengeful cruelty, she'd accepted his triumphant assessment.

Not now, she thought grimly. Now she'd see him in court so fast he'd get skid marks. But then she'd been foolishly innocent, and the thought of telling anyone what had happened had filled her with shamed horror. A thought struck her, and she added hastily, 'And anyway, he was dead.' More lies.

'It never occurred to you to have an abortion?'

'I didn't realise I was pregnant until just before the May holidays.' She hesitated, then went on, 'I was often irregular. And when I did realise—I was very depressed, still in shock, still trying to deny it. I knew there was no way I could—we could—' She stopped and regained control of her tumbling thoughts. 'Refusing to see you any more seemed the only thing to do.'

Sunk into a nadir of depression, Kate hadn't even been able to grieve. Patric had been lost to her from the night she'd been raped, because it was his cousin who'd attacked her.

'I see.' He sounded detached and thoughtful, his striking face revealing no emotion.

He was possibly a little disappointed that he didn't have a son—most men wanted one—but no doubt he was also grateful that his uncomplicated life would remain that way.

'Could you take me home, please?' Kate asked, stiffening her shoulders against waves of tiredness.

He said inflexibly, 'You look exhausted. Stay and have some dinner, and then I'll take you back.'

Kate glanced at her watch—only seven-thirty. Nick would still be awake, and for once she didn't feel up to coping with him. 'I don't want...I'm not hungry, Patric.'

'I've ordered a meal,' he said. 'Eating something will make you feel better.'

Only time could do that.

For years she'd managed to ignore her intellectual acceptance of Nick's paternity; until she'd seen Patric at the theme park she hadn't realised that in some hidden, resistant part of her heart she'd always pretended he was the father of her son.

How stupid to let her heart fool her like that! Now that her delusion had been exposed to the hard light of day it had brutally turned on her, inflicting the kind of pain she'd hoped never to suffer again.

With dark, masked eyes Patric said quietly, 'Let's sit at the table.'

Somehow the normal process of dining—sitting down, unfolding the napkin, watching him ladle out soup, picking up her spoon—steadied her, reminded her that, whatever happened, life went on.

'You must have found it difficult looking after Nick on a government benefit,' Patric said. 'Did your aunt and uncle help?'

The iced avocado soup was delicious, based on real chicken stock, Kate thought vaguely, dipping her spoon into the creamy pale green liquid. 'They couldn't; for a couple of years they really struggled in Rarotonga. Anyway, they thought I was crazy keeping him. They wanted me to adopt him out.'

'Why didn't you?'

Searching for the right words, she drank some more soup. 'Several reasons,' she said eventually. 'I'd grown up in someone else's family. Oh, they tried very hard, but I always felt the odd person out. I didn't want that for Nick. But the main reason was that when he was born—he looked just like me. It would have been like giving myself away, and I couldn't do it.'

'Did you tell your aunt and uncle that you were attacked?' he asked.

She shook her head. 'What was the use? It would only have made them wretched. I didn't even tell them about the baby until after I had him.'

'You had him alone?' he asked, looking at her with glints of cold blue in his dark eyes.

'When I dropped out of university—after the May holidays—I stayed in Christchurch and kept house for two dentists. They were good to me—took me to the hospital, visited me. Before I had Nick I'd organised a flat in Whangarei, and saved up enough money to travel to get there. We arrived when he was three weeks old.'

His brows drew together in a formidable frown. 'To all intents and purposes you were alone. Who do your family think Nick's father is?'

'I've never said.'

Surprisingly, he allowed her to get away with the evasion. Perhaps he didn't recognise it. She should have been reassured, but her hand trembled as she picked up her spoon again.

'I'm sorry,' Patric said unexpectedly.

'For what?'

'For—everything.'

Kate hadn't forgotten—she doubted whether anyone

ever forgot being raped—but she had long ago come to terms with it. Proudly she said, 'I refused to make myself a victim, so I left it behind me.'

'Very wise,' he said, a disturbing note beneath the words making her look up. But there was nothing to be read in his face, no emotion visible in his unwavering eyes as he finished, 'And strong-minded.'

'Just sensible.'

When the plates were empty in front of them Patric said, 'I'll get the second course.'

Kate opened her mouth to protest, then fleetingly met eyes as opaque as polished granite and every bit as obdurate. 'You're determined to feed me, aren't you?' she said, trying to speak lightly.

'It's the least I can do after subjecting you to such an inquisition.'

Her brows pleated as he got up, collected the soup plates, and walked from the table into the kitchen. Tall, lithe, his well-knit body vibrated with a breath-catching male beauty. Something hidden and feline stirred inside her, stretched languorously, flowed through her with a smooth, primal insistence.

Desperately, Kate dragged her gaze away. Patric had opened the long doors onto a wide terrace bordered with potted palms. Fresh and familiar, a salty breeze stirred the curtains. Through the palm fronds the sand glinted in the light of a rising moon; movement and shadows indicated that people were still walking along the beach. The sound of the sea filled the room, a quiet thunder echoed by her heart.

An ache of yearning broke over her, submerged her— sweet, inexorable, merciless, a honeyed hunger leaching into her endurance. It had been so long, and her taste of loving had been so brief, snatched away by an act of callous violence...

And that's enough of that, she told herself, stiffening her spine. You have a good life, and once this interlude with Patric is over you'll be able to settle back into it. If you meet a man you can fall in love with, one who'll love Nick as much as he would a son of his own, then you might consider changing it.

'The menu says the asparagus comes from New Zealand,' Patric said, carrying a tray to the table. 'I assume you still like it?'

Kate looked down at racks of tiny lamb chops, long straight spears of asparagus, glistening darkly green under a golden veil of butter, and small, round new potatoes, white, voluptuous and tender.

'I adore it,' she said, intolerably shaken that he'd remembered. Hastily seizing on a neutral aspect, she went on, 'I didn't know we exported asparagus to Australia.'

'Along with a multitude of other things,' he said.

At once stimulated and wary, Kate soon responded to Patric's incisive comments on the latest political scandal, contradicting him and then enjoying the resultant sparring so much that for a precious time she forgot all that stood between them. In Kate's life there was little opportunity for leisurely talk of any kind, let alone a free-ranging analysis of world events, of books, ideas and films.

At length, when they'd both eaten everything on their plates, he said, 'I gather you've not finished your degree.'

She gave a quick shake of her head.

'Are you doing subjects extramurally?' he asked.

It sounded almost like an accusation. 'No,' she said, sitting up straighter.

He lifted his brows. 'Why not?'

'I don't have the money,' she said crisply, adding, 'Or the time.'

'A brain as good as yours should be exercised, and I don't imagine that working in a dress shop in Whangarei gives you much intellectual stimulation. Nor Nick's conversation, however charming he is. There are limits to a six-year-old's depth.' He paused, then added coolly, 'Unless you have someone else to talk to.'

Turbulence swirled beneath the dark voice, like an off-shore rip coiling under innocently smooth water.

Kate's mouth dried. 'I read a lot—Whangarei has an excellent library. And I have friends, and very good neighbours,' she parried. 'Anna and Jacob are in their eighties, Germans who fled the Holocaust and somehow landed up in Whangarei. They adore discussions on almost anything. Anna spoils Nick and Jacob gives him a piano lesson for ten minutes every day. He taught him how to play the mouth organ too.'

'How good is Nick?'

'On the piano?' She smiled. 'Jacob says he has talent but no genius; at the moment all he's doing is enjoying himself. He can play three tunes on the mouth organ, though, so he's now convinced he's an expert.'

Patric laughed. Low and totally self-assured, it was the laugh of a man who has everything in the world he wants—or who is positive of his ability to get it. The young Kate had been dazzled by that confidence; perhaps because she'd always felt an outsider she'd been sure she needed accomplishments to pay her way.

'He obviously has a wide range of interests,' Patric observed, pouring a glass of water for her.

Her gaze lingered on his hands—lean and sinewy and graceful. And gentle, she thought suddenly. Patric's hands had been so gentle—and then they had been harsh, and she had shivered with pleasure at both the gentleness and the harshness...

Dragging her mind back from perilous memories, she said, 'He gets fascinated by something and wants to know all about it—sort of plunges into it. I'm already an expert on spiders and lizards and how mouth organs work. When Nick gets interested, he demands more and more information, soaking it up long after everyone else is bored to screaming point.'

'And at the moment it's birds.'

'Yes. We've read books from the library about birds,

and listened to bird calls, and watched birds and collected their feathers and pasted them into a notebook—you name it, we've done it. But soon he'll become absorbed in something new and it will start all over again. Sometimes I think he's got a butterfly mind.'

'Hardly,' Patric said. He'd poured wine, a good Australian red, but had left it untouched. Now he drank some down. When he put the glass back on the table he tilted it, so that the liquid caught the light and flashed crimson, his dark eyes concealed by the thick fringe of lashes. 'He seems to explore deeply as well as widely. I remember my grandmother telling me that ''Black'' Pat was like that. The only thing that ever kept his attention was Sutherland Aviation.' He set the glass straight on the table and looked at her with half-closed eyes. 'It will be intriguing to see what Nick grows up like. Why did you call him Nicholas?'

'It was my father's name,' she said carefully. Nick's second name was Patrick—another instance of the delusion she'd cherished. And if Nick had inherited anything from 'Black Pat' Sutherland it had not descended through Patric.

'I'd like to have known your father. Do you and Nick look like him?'

'No, we look like my mother.'

'She must have been a great beauty.'

Kate smiled mistily. 'I don't remember her, of course—I was only three when they died—but judging by photographs she was much better looking than I am.'

He lifted his brows. 'I find that hard to believe. Did she have your astonishing eyes?' An iron-grey glance lingered a second on her mouth.

A slow shimmer of heat smouldered through Kate. Quickly, before it flared into wildfire, she said, 'She had a glory about her, a kind of radiance that shone right through the camera lens and onto paper. I wish I'd known her.'

'Why was she climbing Mount Everest when she had a small child?' he asked, frowning.

'According to Aunt Jean, my parents intended having another baby, so my mother decided to try Everest before she did. Both she and my father were born climbers. In a way it was fitting that they died there.'

'No wonder Nick likes the thrill of roller-coasters,' Patric said sardonically.

'Those genes skipped a generation. I don't like danger.'

'Really?' His smile was tinged with mockery. 'Yet I've always thought you were incredibly dangerous—even when you were fourteen—with those huge, vulnerable eyes and that passionate mouth, and skin like pale gold silk. You scared me silly, and as you grew into your beauty it became harder and harder to remember that you were six years younger than I was. And in the end I gave up trying to.'

'I'm a very ordinary person,' she objected, trying to keep her head.

'And yet you'd say that Nick is a handsome child.'

She hesitated, then admitted, 'Well, yes, but I'm allowed to be biased—I'm his mother. To me he's perfect.'

'He's a handsome boy who looks just like you.' He watched with heavy-lashed eyes as colour burnt through her skin. 'Although he doesn't look vulnerable. He has strong bones.'

His eyelids drooped further, hiding his thoughts. The light above the table played warmly across the autocratic angles and planes of his face, emphasising sweeping cheekbones, an uncompromising jaw and the surprising beauty of his mouth. No vulnerability there, Kate thought acidly, nor any innocence; he'd probably been born so-phisticated, and his face revealed nothing but disciplined power.

Disconcertingly his lashes lifted, and she realised that he'd been watching her through them.

Sensation speared through her, clean and sharp and

piercing. She felt it in her suddenly heavy breasts; it cramped her womb and tightened her skin, warning her that she was heading into hazardous waters.

Patric got to his feet, startling her afresh with his height and the width of his shoulders. 'There's pudding,' he said casually. 'A mango concoction.'

'It sounds lovely.'

Now that he knew Nick wasn't his she'd never see him again; she could allow herself a few more minutes of this perilous pleasure.

While he collected the used plates and went into the kitchen, she tried to control the high beating of her heart in her throat, the singing tide of need that surged through every cell, the swift clutch of desire in the pit of her stomach.

Sexual hunger was simply a matter of chemistry—inconvenient, meaning little.

Except that she had never felt it for another man. And had never wanted to.

That first act of love all those years ago—and the subsequent brutal assault—had somehow frozen her responses. She wasn't afraid of men, and she was thankful that she'd made love with Patric first, so she'd known the glory of fulfilled desire instead of being initiated into debasement. But until she'd seen him again and felt excitement storm through her in a wild clamour she hadn't responded physically to a man.

And instead of asking herself why, she'd gratefully accepted celibacy.

Now, as she heard Patric moving quietly about the kitchen, she wondered why she'd been content to dream the years away, to ignore any overtures that came her way, to live a sexless life.

Perhaps she should thank Patric for waking her again, she thought painfully as he came back into the room.

'Mango mousse,' he said, sliding the container in front of her.

The pale contents of the elegant bowl were decorated with an elaborate swirl of chocolate in three shades.

'Where did you get such superb food?' she asked, grateful for the opportunity to ignore her thoughts.

'One of the local restaurants does a delivery service. Would you like to serve me some?'

She spooned the delicious stuff onto a plate and handed it to him, then put out a small amount for herself. It was magnificent—not too sweet, not too rich—and the chocolate shavings added a luscious touch of contrast in texture and flavour.

'Lovely,' Kate said on a slow sigh of pleasure when the first mouthful had eased down her appreciative throat. 'My compliments to the chef.'

'I'll make sure he gets them,' Patric promised. 'Eat up before it gets too warm.'

In the clipped words she heard a sudden roughness, as though he disliked the situation, but when she looked up he smiled, and at that smile—warm, a little coaxing—she knew she'd been imagining things.

After demolishing the mousse with delicate greed, she found herself agreeing to coffee. While he prepared it she got up and walked across to the windows. The moon had risen fully and was now a great white globe in the black sky, its light washing out most of the stars.

Patric had overshadowed all other men for her. Even though she hadn't loved him in the mature way that led to adult happiness, he'd blotted out the impact of any other man.

Well, that could stop right now. Oh, she still found him sinfully, threateningly attractive, but she wasn't going to spend the rest of her life mourning a youthful romance.

Or losing herself in inchoate fantasies where he was the father of her child, instead of the real father—a man who'd raped her because she was Patric's girlfriend, because he'd hated and envied Patric all his life, a man who'd laughed at her frantic struggles until she'd managed to deliver several blows to a vulnerable spot.

Then he'd held a knife to her throat, and when it was done he'd called her trash, and gloated that if she ever saw his cousin again he'd tell Patric he'd had her—describe how she'd moaned and twisted in his arms, lie about every sordid, horrifying detail as though she'd wanted him instead of fighting him almost to a standstill.

Even now, years later, she had to breathe a residue of panic away and remind herself that Patric could lead his cousin to Nick.

When she'd decided to keep her son she'd been terrified that his father's cruelty might be hereditary; she'd tried to give Nick a happy, satisfying life, with no need to express himself in aggression and malice. And she'd succeeded. He was sunny-natured—strong-willed too, but he was learning that although loyalty to friends was a good quality, sympathy and understanding of those he didn't like so much was important too.

He would never—*never*—know who his father was and what he'd done. If she had to spend the rest of her life on the run, she'd see that Sean never found out he'd fathered a child on her. But to make sure of that she'd have to persuade Patric never to tell anyone he'd seen her again.

As Patric came into the room with a tray she said, 'Can I have your promise that what I've told you tonight won't go any further?'

He bent to set the tray down on the table between the sofa and the chair. Lamplight gleamed on the blue-black depths of his hair, washed over his arrogant nose and the square chin.

When he stood up she could see that he was angry. 'I don't usually break confidences,' he said arctically.

'I'm talking about Nick.' She paused to gather strength. 'I'm not going to tell him who his father was or the circumstances of his conception. When he's older he might find out that—that you and I saw a lot of each other that summer. He might even track you down. I don't want you to lie to him, but could you simply say that you're not his father and that you don't know who is?'

'I could do that,' he said steadily, scanning her face with opaque, impersonal eyes. 'But he's going to resent your silence.'

She bit her lip. 'I've told him his father is dead.'

'What will you do when he begins to ask more detailed questions?'

'I don't know,' she admitted, 'but that's my problem, not yours.'

'All right,' he said deliberately, 'I won't tell him you were raped.'

Stiffly Kate said, 'Thank you. And—could you not tell anyone you've seen me? I don't want any reminders of the past cluttering up my life.' She made it a command rather than a plea.

His brows knitted, then smoothed out; she met the hard impact of his eyes with what she hoped was cool self-possession.

'Of course,' he said after a noticeable pause, and added, 'Come and pour some coffee. Would you like a brandy?'

She hadn't touched the wine he'd poured for her, and apart from that once he hadn't drunk any of his, either.

'No, thank you,' she said, glad of the excuse to walk back to the sofa and sit down; her legs felt as though the stuffing had been taken from them. Carefully she poured his coffee—black and sugarless, just as he liked it—and handed it to him.

They talked quietly, trying to burnish some sort of civ-ilised gloss on an evening that had put them both through an emotional wringer. Kate cast a covert glance at the man beside her, long legs sprawled in front of him as he drank his coffee. What was he thinking?

It was impossible to tell. Even when he'd been growing up Patric's face had told the world only what he'd wanted it to know.

CHAPTER FOUR

On the way back to her apartment Patric asked, 'When do you really leave for New Zealand?'

Shame tripped Kate's tongue. 'On Friday.'

He gave her a quick, slicing look. 'It's all right, Kate. I won't harass you, but I don't want to lose sight of you again. We had fun all those years ago, didn't we?'

'Yes, but...'

At her hesitation he supplied drily, 'But we're two different people now. Still, you enjoyed tonight—parts of it, anyway.'

Troubled by a shadowy foreboding, she said, 'Yes, I did.'

'Don't sound so surprised. I did too.' His voice was reflective. 'I've almost tied up my business here, and I don't have to be back in New Zealand for another couple of days. Can we at least pick up the threads of our friendship?'

Excitement warred with caution, almost banishing her fears in a hot blaze of fascination. Don't be a coward, a voice purred. What harm can it do? If nothing else it might finally end those foolish, infantile hopes and dreams you've been carrying around for so long.

And he'd promised not to tell anyone he'd met her again. Patric didn't break promises.

Yet she said, 'You can never go back, Patric—life doesn't work that way.'

'I know.' He spoke calmly, almost meditatively. 'Going back is impossible, but I would like to go forward.'

The very simplicity of his words crashed through her

defences as nothing else could have. 'Yes,' she said quietly, 'I'd like that too.'

He didn't touch her, but she felt his glance, and his voice was warm as he said, 'Thank you.'

Again that fleeting, baseless apprehension whispered across her skin.

Patric asked, 'What is it?'

He'd always had an uncanny way of seeing far more than she wanted him to. Once she'd hoped it meant that they were psychically linked; now she thought it was probably an inbuilt understanding of body language, honed by his brilliant brain into a weapon. No doubt it came in very useful in his business life.

She said, 'Someone walked over my grave.'

Through the side window she stared at tourists laughing and playing and calling to each other in a streetscape that danced and dazzled, lights and music a garish counterpoint to the wide, white beach and the limitless sea beyond the buildings and the cafés and the ubiquitous palms.

'You never used to be superstitious,' Patric said.

Her smile was tinged with bitterness. 'I never used to be a lot of things.'

The unspoken past was suddenly with them, rich with memories, each one saturated with delight and the heady potency of first love—and the pain that had followed.

'How bad was it?' Patric asked, his voice harsh.

'I managed.' Why tell him that the girl she'd been had died, that for years the only thing that had kept her going was Nick's utter dependence on her? She'd struggled free of that dreary winter of the soul. It was over, over and done with.

'I wish I'd known,' he said roughly.

'It wasn't your—'

'I'd have helped you. No woman should have to go through such trauma—and then bear and bring up a child—on her own.'

Kate squelched a debilitating hope by saying, 'Your wife might not have approved.'

Was it her imagination, or did the long fingers tense a moment on the wheel?

He said remotely, 'Laura and I didn't have a particularly close relationship.'

Stupid to feel dismissed, like an impertinent schoolgirl! Just as distantly Kate returned, 'It never occurred to me to contact you,' only realising when she'd said the words that she'd tried to hurt him as he'd hurt her.

Before he could answer, if he'd intended to, she asked lightly, 'How are your family—your mother and your aunt?' Greatly daring, she added, 'And what happened to your obnoxious cousin?'

'Sean?' He said the name as though it tasted foul. 'We don't see him any more. I haven't spoken to him for the last two years, and I have no intention of ever speaking to him again. I don't know where he is, but he won't be coming back to New Zealand.'

Thank God. Oh, thank God! Banishing the wild relief from her voice, she said, 'Your mother?'

'She's fine.' He didn't hesitate—it was impossible to think of Patric hesitating—but he paused before he said, 'She divides her time between Europe and New Zealand now, with side trips to various places.'

'It sounds a wonderful life.'

'She enjoys it.' Killing the engine beneath the sheltering portico at the apartment block, Patric said, 'Where are you planning to go tomorrow?'

'The last theme park,' she said, adding with a wry smile, 'More roller-coasters.'

His quiet laugh was suffocatingly intimate in the confines of the car. 'I like roller-coasters.'

Was he inviting himself along? Kate's heart jumped and she tried to ignore a slow, tantalising glimpse of delight. It would be perilously sweet to spend a day with him, especially as Nick would be the perfect buffer. And she no longer had to worry about Sean.

Striving to be practical, she realised also that if Patric came she wouldn't have to endure any more nail-biting, white-knuckled rides on assorted torture-machines.

But it wasn't pragmatism that persuaded her to say, 'If you don't mind spending the whole day having your stomach turned upside down, you're welcome to come too.'

'Would Nick mind?' he asked.

'Why should he?'

'Some children—boys especially, and even more so if they haven't got a father—are inclined to be possessive of their mothers.'

'Nick's not like that.' He'd had no opportunity—there had never been another man.

Patric nodded. 'What time will I pick you up?'

'The park opens at ten, so we'd better be there soon afterwards. Patric, are you sure you'd like it? Nick is a tiger for punishment, and we usually go all day. It's kids' stuff.'

'I was a kid once. I'll be here at a quarter to ten,' he said, and got out of the car.

She'd expected him to leave her at the main entrance. However, waiting for the lifts were a group of young men, obviously enjoying their first adult holiday. When she opened the door Patric strode in behind her.

They weren't rude or obnoxious, merely noisy and just too openly appreciative. Nevertheless, without saying a word, Patric made it more than clear that she was under his protection. And they accepted it, giving ground before the alpha male.

Men, Kate thought. In spite of the efforts of their mothers, and other assorted females through the ages, they still operated on primitive principles.

The babysitter was waiting inside the unit. As Kate lifted her purse from her bag, Patric handed over a banknote.

The babysitter looked at it. 'I haven't got change.'

'It's not necessary,' he said. 'Can I drive you home?'

Kate opened her mouth to object, then closed it again. She'd pay him back when the sitter had gone.

'No, thanks, I've got my car here.' She glanced from one to the other, gave them both a wide smile, and left, saying, 'He was a perfect kid, no problem at all. Goodnight.'

Awkwardly Kate closed the door behind her. 'How much was it?' she asked, fishing money from her purse.

Patric's gunmetal gaze was impossible to read. 'Humour me, Kate. You wouldn't have needed her if I hadn't pressed you to go out with me.'

'Well, no— but...'

He closed her fingers over the notes in her hand. As his touch ricocheted through her, every cell in her body burst into clamorous life. Her breath died in her throat.

Something flared in the depths of his eyes. 'I don't want your money. Buy Nick a souvenir or some new clothes.' The inflexible words were modified by a raw undercurrent that set her senses jangling. He released her hand and stepped back.

After a moment her pulses calmed down enough for her to say numbly, 'Thank you. I'll just check him.'

He was sleeping soundly, sprawled out across the sheets and blanket, the muted light from a lamp outside kindling hidden fire in his hair. Desperately trying to recover, Kate bent to touch his cheek, noting the steady rise and fall of his chest, and her heart clenched with sudden, overpowering love.

Unconsciously she passed her hand over his hair, and he stirred and said in a blurry voice, 'Mummy?'

'Yes, it's me. Go back to sleep,' she said softly.

He muttered something before relapsing into slumber. Kate waited, but he didn't move again. After straightening his sheet she turned away, only taking one step before she collided with a solid body.

'Oh!' Heat, she thought dazedly, stepping back, jerking free of Patric's swift grip on her elbows so quickly she almost tripped. Heat from his body—from her own—enveloped her.

She'd forgotten his faint male scent, so evocative that it bypassed her senses and homed straight to her emotions. Owing nothing to aftershave, it was the essence of the man who was Patric Sutherland—masculine, sexual, redolent of his energy and dynamic power and discipline, his keen mind and his effortless, understated authority.

It set her heart afire, roused her senses and magically, dangerously, switched off the insistent, cautious prompting of her brain. Drowning in an urgency of physical need, she had to get out of there fast.

So she had to walk. Now.

'Kate?' he asked quietly.

'It's all right,' she muttered.

On wobbly legs she retreated out of the room and down the lighted hallway while Patric closed the bedroom door behind him. Obeying an imperative warning, Kate headed to the front door and opened it.

'Goodnight,' she said.

'Goodnight.' His voice was cool and deep and emotionless, but when he reached her he stopped and smiled—a smile that stopped Kate's heart.

'You're even more beautiful,' he said, and touched her mouth with a lean forefinger. 'The eyes of a siren and the pride of a lioness, hair like black silk dusted with fire, and a mouth that suggests promises I'd kill to collect on.'

Desire smoked through the words, stark, relentless, overwhelming her. His smile took over her mind as she closed the door behind him and leaned back against it, stupid, unwanted tears filling her eyes as her heart thudded erratically against her breastbone.

Their day at the theme park was a time of complicated, reckless pleasure. Patric rode every ride with Nick, sealing her son's affection and respect, and answered constant questions with faultless patience and what seemed to be true interest. Even when Nick became tired and a little grumpy his tolerance didn't waver.

Amusing, protective and masterful in a low-key way, formal clothes banished for a light shirt and casual trousers, those angular, striking features not exactly softened by his good humour, he gave Nick his full attention. And because he possessed a natural talent for leadership, Nick became an enthusiastic follower. Patric's hard eyes gentled when they rested on her son's face, and he joined Nick in teasing her because she refused to terrify herself into fits.

As she made a spirited defence Kate caught herself thinking how wonderful it would be to have someone to share the responsibility. It seemed shameful, as though she'd put Patric—with his broad shoulders, his ability to conjure waitresses and his compelling authority—before Nick.

Afterwards, when her son was asleep, Kate sat down on the side of her bed, listening to the silence of the apartment. That day, beguiled by an old, sentimental dream, she'd surrendered to the magic Patric had always been able to weave about her.

But once they got on the plane to New Zealand it would be over. He was a busy man—far too busy to have time to spare for a woman who'd once jilted him and a boy without a father.

The telephone rang. Starting, Kate stared at it before reaching out to pick it up. Her fingers, she noted, were shaking. Although she'd known who it would be, her bones melted at the sound of Patric's voice.

'I hoped you wouldn't be in bed,' he said.

'I'm on my way.'

'Are you tired?'

Kate seized the excuse. 'Actually, I am,' she said, keeping her voice light. 'I thought it was steeling myself to go on those wretched rides that wears me out, but it must be the parks themselves.' She made herself finish, 'Patric, thank you so much. Nick had a glorious time.'

There was a moment's silence. 'Did you have a good time too?'

'Yes, of course.'

'But Nick comes first.'

Kate said firmly, 'He has to.'

'I understand.' His voice altered slightly as he went on, 'He's a great kid. Did we ever have that much energy?'

Her mouth curved spontaneously. 'Oh, I think so,' she said. 'When we were young.'

Quiet laughter sent shivers up her spine. 'So long ago,' he mocked. 'I remember the day we all went to Raglan for a picnic—do you?'

Her heart lurched; he'd kissed her for the very first time that day, gently, tenderly, and she'd gone up like a sky-rocket as they'd stood, wet skin against wet skin, hearts beating so intensely that their subdued thunder still resounded in her ears. It had been her first experience of the merciless power of passion.

'I remember,' she said drily. How quickly he'd accustomed her to the slow, sweet, almost chaste caresses that were all he'd allowed himself that summer.

Of course he'd had a very willing pupil. Rapidly she asked, 'Why did you ring, Patric?'

'To say goodnight,' he said, his voice indolently amused. 'And to thank you.'

She should have left it at that, but she didn't. 'What for?'

'For letting me come with you today.'

A supplicant attitude was not a natural one for Patric. Uneasily wondering whether he was up to anything, Kate said, 'We had a super time, didn't we? I hope Nick thanked you.'

'Several times—he has excellent manners. What would you like to do tomorrow? You've run out of theme parks.'

'Yes, that was the last today.'

'Would Nick like to go to a lighthouse? There's a little one just over the border in New South Wales, where the waves roar in onto the rocks with a very satisfying crash and hiss of spray. Afterwards we could go to the top of Mount Tamborine and watch the hang-gliders take off.'

'Nick would love it,' she said slowly. 'Thank you.'

'Would you like it?'

A little bewildered, she answered, 'Yes, of course.'

'Right. I'll pick you up at nine.' He waited a second, then finished easily, 'Goodnight, Kate. Dream of good things.'

She murmured an answer and hung up. If only she could separate the past from the present, but whenever he spoke in that tone—whenever he smiled at her, whenever his dark gaze rested on her face—she was once more the child who'd loved him, made love with him and lost him.

One more day, she promised herself, getting into bed. That's all. And it is wonderful for Nick to have a male companion like Patric, even if it's only for a short time.

Her son knew plenty of men, but seldom had the unadulterated attention of one for any length of time. So this was for Nick. She turned out the light and went to sleep, to dream of Patric.

Kate flushed the next morning when she recalled those dreams, but Patric's behaviour that day reassured her. Because he was Patric he was sexy and wildly attractive, but there was nothing remotely sexual—or even gallant— in his attitude. For which she was grateful, she told herself.

She wasn't in the least bit irritated that Nick thought the sun shone through those dark grey eyes. Not a bit. And certainly not jealous.

Not even when Nick's every second sentence began with *Mr Sutherland says*.

The lighthouse was glorious—a cute, white, two-storeyed affair on a headland. An island crouched offshore, and through trees they could see a long, wave-pounded beach stretching to a cluster of hazy towers that denoted another seaside resort.

'Did you notice,' Kate said, 'that once you get over the border into New South Wales there are no palms?'

Patric laughed. 'Yes, I'd noticed.'

'So did I,' Nick said loyally.

They grinned at each other, and Nick suddenly hugged them both, twining his arms around their waists. 'We look like a family,' he said with satisfaction. 'I bet those people over there think we're a proper family. I'm sorry you haven't got any children, Mr Sutherland. If you had, I could play with them. Can we go and see the waves now, Mummy?'

Shaken, Kate said, 'Yes.'

'There's no beach beneath the cliffs,' Patric told him, 'So we have to stand well back. All right?'

Nick nodded, a little in awe of the cool authority in Patric's tone. They walked across the tawny grass and stood watching the rounded waves surge in and smash themselves against the rocks in a smother of spray. The impact throbbed through the ground like the dynamo of some hidden power source.

'Look!' Nick breathed, taking a few steps towards the edge of the cliff.

'Why don't you sit against that screw pine?' Patric suggested. 'You'll be able to see the foam burst above the rocks very clearly from there.'

Obediently, Nick sat on the grass, leaning back against the trunk, and stared with wide eyes at the waves.

'Do you think he might have found the next big interest?' Patric asked.

'It looks like it.'

With his eyes fixed on the smooth, humped combers coming in, and the wild outburst of spray, Patric said, 'Laura didn't want children.'

Torn between a need to know what had happened and an immense reluctance to hear anything about his marriage, Kate hesitated before saying, 'That's a shame, if you wanted them.'

He gave her a brief, unsmiling look. Another breaker thudded into the black rocks, sending a wild fountain of spray into the air, white foam against the intense ultramarine of the sea. 'It never occurred to me that we wouldn't have them. Marrying Laura was the most spectacularly stupid thing I've ever done.'

'Then why did you do it?'

'Her father was my father's greatest friend.' His voice was cool, almost bored, but the note of distaste in the words chilled her; he turned his head so that all she could see were the angles of his profile. 'I liked her and I knew she liked me. What I didn't know was that both my father and Laura's were desperate for me to marry her.'

Kate had been sure she'd overcome her disconcerting tendency to jealousy, but even to hear him say Laura's name ate like acid into her composure. 'You don't have to tell me this,' she said, the words pinched and abrupt.

'I think I do. I'd have preferred a less public place— although perhaps it's a good thing it's not.'

She said nothing, keeping her eyes fixed on a group of girls who'd just walked by with a couple of teachers and some long-suffering parents. A few feet away Nick crouched, mesmerised.

After a moment Patric went on, 'My father wanted to see me married, settled before he died.'

'I can understand that.'

Apparently irrelevantly he said, 'He loved Tatamoa, loved farming, the whole agricultural scene. He only took over Sutherland Aviation because it would have broken ''Black'' Pat's heart to see it sold.'

Kate nodded.

Patric's voice was calm, reflective. 'He wasn't a spectacular failure—he was a hard-working, reliable, conscientious managing director—but he had little understanding of business and a tendency to trust the wrong people.

When I took over Sutherland's it was perilously close to going under. It needed radical restructuring, and I had to work with a board my father had packed with men who were sure I was heading in the wrong direction. Laura's father was on it; he was the only one who understood what I wanted to do. The others trusted him, so he had the power to bring them around.'

Kate said tightly, 'You married Laura to haul Sutherland Aviation out of the fire? Pull the other leg, Patric. That sort of thing died with the Victorians.'

His mouth thinned. 'How innocent you are, Kate.' It wasn't a compliment. 'Of course no one actually came out and stated it—the pressure was subtle. I was grieving for my father, supporting my mother as best I could, and working furiously to save several thousand jobs around the world, so I didn't immediately take in the full implications.' After a taut moment he continued, 'I married Laura because I was forced to.'

Patric—determined, resolute, strong-willed Patric— forced to do something against his will? *Marry* against his will? Kate's disbelief was mirrored in her face, in the scornful twist of her mouth.

He answered her unspoken question. 'Hard to credit, I'll agree, but one tends to want to do what one can for one's dying father. Not marry to order, however. As soon as I realised what my father was pushing for I went to see Laura.'

'And?' She remembered how Laura used to look at him.

Broad shoulders moved in the slightest of shrugs. 'She thought it an excellent idea. She was ready to settle down, she said, and we knew each other well. It would make both our fathers happy, and help mine die in peace. It would also help Sutherland Aviation when it became known that her father was backing me.'

'How sensible of her.'

Patric's laugh was low and caustic. 'I'm afraid I offended her with my reaction. I had to see you, so I came down to Tatamoa.'

Kate closed her eyes briefly.

'I was going to ask you to marry me,' he said levelly, 'But you told me you no longer wanted anything to do with me, and that you had another lover. I was so stunned I couldn't think, couldn't do anything but fight to control my instinct to snatch you up and keep you with me until you admitted that you loved me.' His words were textured by self-contempt. 'My fury and panic frightened me and shocked me. I hated losing control, so I thought I'd give you until the end of the year.

'About ten minutes after I got back to Auckland from Poto still in shock because you'd said you didn't want anything more to do with me, Laura rang. She said she'd decided to inform our parents that she was pregnant to me. If that didn't persuade me to marry her, she'd tell them she was going to have an abortion. She knew what that would do to my parents—especially my father, who'd always wanted a big family.'

In the pockets of her jeans Kate's hands clenched so tightly she could feel the pain in her knuckles. It was easier to bear than the pain in her heart. 'Was she pregnant?'

'No, and if she had been it wouldn't have been mine. We'd never slept together. We had an argument. I told her to keep away from my parents, and then I flew down to Christchurch to find you, but you'd already left the university and disappeared. While I was there my father had to be rushed into hospital—it was touch and go for thirty-six hours. A week later, when he was well enough to come home, I rang your aunt and uncle. But they'd gone too.'

'They were given a handsome payment and a week to get off the place,' she said, thin-lipped. Another wave crashed onto the black rocks, its impact reverberating through the ground as foam soared high into the air.

Patric's striking buccaneer's face hardened. 'I was told your uncle had resigned.'

'He was sacked.'

He swore beneath his breath, his voice flat and lethal. 'My father wasn't the businessman that "Black" Pat was, but he could be every bit as ruthless. That was when Laura's father told me he'd see Sutherland Aviation go down if I didn't marry her. She stayed away from my parents, but she'd convinced him that she was pregnant with my child.'

'What did your mother think of all this?' It hurt that Mrs Sutherland, whom Kate had always liked, should have allowed her son to be blackmailed into marriage.

'She wasn't happy, but I suspect she had a desperate hope that a grandchild might give my father an extra reason to live.'

He was hating this, and so was Kate. Long-dormant emotions churned through her, setting fire to her temper like sparks in the wind. How could his parents have used his love and respect to force him into a marriage he didn't want?

Watching her son, Kate said in a low, furious voice, 'They should be ashamed of themselves, all of them.'

'Laura's father lost his daughter,' Patric said unemotionally. 'My father died, leaving my mother a widow. Laura died. I think they all paid, don't you?'

'What about you?' she asked passionately. 'They betrayed you.'

'After you told me you didn't want to see me any more and then disappeared I no longer cared much,' he said smoothly. 'I knew what the crash of Sutherland Aviation would do to my father, and to the people who were working for it.'

Guilt reined in her anger. 'Their pressure must have been almost unbearable. And you loved your father.'

'Oh, yes,' he said with remote precision. 'At least he was dead before it came totally unstuck. Laura wanted a playmate, and what she got was a man driven to work day and night to rescue what I could from the wreckage my father had inadvertently left.

'She waited until after my father died to announce that she'd had a miscarriage.' He swung around and directed an oblique, unreadable glance at her. 'So that's the sad story of my marriage,' he said, bare steel ringing through each word. 'Two years later Laura drank too much one night when I was overseas and went for a swim. She drowned.'

Nobody deserved to die like that, but Laura had certainly asked for unhappiness.

'I'm sorry,' Kate said, meaning it. 'I wonder why we have to make decisions when we're in the worst possible state to see clearly.'

'To test us, perhaps.' He looked down at Nick, who was utterly absorbed in watching the waves come in. 'Seen enough?'

'He won't hear you—he's lost in wonder.' Kate took the few steps to the screw pine and bent down. 'Come on, Nick, it's time to go.'

'Oh.' He scrambled up, his face radiant. 'Mummy, where do the waves come from? How do they build up? Why do they get white tops on them? Is it steam?'

'No, it's foam, and we'll look up the answers to your other questions when we get back home,' Kate said, smiling as the wind tossed her hair about her face. Patric's story had affected her profoundly but she couldn't deal with it now.

He said, 'It looks like you have another project on your hands.'

'Are we going for a swim off that beach?' Nick asked.

'It's too rough,' Kate said firmly. 'We'll wait until we get back to the apartments. However, Mr Sutherland says he knows where there are some hang-gliders.'

They spent the afternoon on top of Mount Tamborine, watching hang-gliders launch themselves and soar across a valley the colour of light toast. Kate, a sensible distance back from the low wall that marked the drop-off, watched closely as Patric took Nick's hand and walked over to the low barrier. After a few moments she relaxed; Patric was well able to curb her son's natural desire to get too close to the cliff-edge.

She allowed herself to take in the glorious gold of the valley below the cliff, the dim blue outline of the Great Dividing Range to the west, and the scent of Australia—dry, exciting, tinged with eucalyptus and smoke.

Nick, small hand lost in Patric's, hopped with eagerness, his voice rising and falling as questions bubbled from him.

Patric answered them all.

After that they had a drink at a café and drove down the winding, steep highway to the Gold Coast.

'We're going home tomorrow,' Nick said from the back. 'A part of our prize is a shuttle. It's just a bus, but it brought us down from the airport and tomorrow it will take us back. We have to be ready at three in the afternoon.'

'What time do you fly out?' Patric asked.

'Qantas leaves at exactly six o'clock.' Nick sighed, then cheered up. 'But we get back to New Zealand in the middle of the night.'

Patric nodded. 'Where are you staying in Auckland?'

'With a friend who lives in Albany,' Kate said. 'She's coming to meet us at the airport.'

'And the next day we're going on the bus to Whangarei,' Nick said importantly.

Patric glanced at Kate. 'I thought you had a car?'

'Not one I'd trust to get me to Auckland and back,' she said crisply.

'We've got an old banger,' Nick informed him with relish. 'It's called Eugene.'

'I remember—a Mini. Why Eugene?'

Kate said, 'That's what its previous owner called it.'

'Once it broke down,' Nick said. 'The radiator cracked and we had to walk everywhere 'til we could save up enough to get it fixed.'

Patric's beautiful mouth tightened fractionally. 'Then you were wise to take the bus to Auckland,' he said.

Feeling like a poor relation, Kate nodded and stared out of the window.

Nick asked, 'When are you going back, Mr Sutherland?'

'Tomorrow too,' he said, 'But not on your plane.'

At the apartments he parked the car in the visitor's slot and said curtly, 'Invite me in, Kate.'

Her hands twisted in her lap. 'I don't think that would be a very good idea,' she said, when the silence had gone on too long.

He switched the engine off. 'I'd like to see how well Nick can swim,' he said, his voice betraying that he knew he was putting her in a difficult situation.

Of course Nick demanded that he stay. Kate gave in, although she was ruffled by Patric's tactics.

'You swim too,' Nick commanded.

He shook his head. 'I haven't got any togs with me. I'll watch you swim.'

Nick didn't need to look quite so disappointed, Kate thought resentfully.

As they sat on the edge of the pool, watching Nick's black head and tanned body, sleek as a seal, while he showed off his prowess, Patric said, 'Don't be angry, Kate.'

'Using Nick like that was unfair, and you know it. It's cruel to play with children's emotions.'

He frowned. 'I hadn't thought of it like that. All right, I won't do it again.'

'Good,' she said curtly, wondering whether that meant he wanted to see more of Nick. If he did, what would she say?

No, she thought swiftly, before temptation set in, it would be too dangerous.

'Come out to dinner with me tonight,' he said indolently.

She shook her head. 'I can't. I have to pack, and to-morrow morning we're going to buy clothes.'

His expression didn't change, but black lashes drooped over eyes the colour of polished iron. 'So this is goodbye,' he said coolly.

Kate kept her eyes on Nick's burnished head. 'Yes.' She knew it had to be said, so why did the word echo through her soul with such cold, implacable finality?

'You're a coward.' Contempt crackled through his voice.

Her own temper fired. 'Because I won't go out to dinner with you? Hardly cowardice, Patric! Just common sense.'

He drawled, 'Your eyes go green as grass when you're angry. What's so sensible about denying yourself a good meal—at a restaurant, if you'd feel safer?'

Kate leaned over and called Nick. 'Come on out,' she said, 'your chin's starting to wobble.'

'Now who's using him?' Patric demanded through his teeth.

Good—he'd lost his temper too. Politely, she said, 'Nick's getting cold. And I don't use him; he's the most important person—the most important thing—in the world to me.'

Complaining, dripping, Nick dragged himself reluctantly up the steps and stood by them as they got to their feet. Still buoyed by anger, Kate said easily, 'Say goodbye to Mr Sutherland, Nick.'

He held out a slim tanned hand and said his farewells. Leashing his temper, Patric shook his hand and said goodbye. Before Kate realised what was happening he bent and took her mouth in a kiss that seared her heart. Her body sprang to life, as though she'd been waiting all these years for that kiss.

When he lifted his head she stared into molten eyes, unable to speak, unable to think, unable to do anything but react.

'Remember that, Sleeping Beauty,' he said in a low,

savage voice, 'When your bed feels empty at night.' And he turned on his heel and walked away.

'Mummy!' Nick tugged at her hand and demanded indignantly, 'Why did he do that?'

Running her tongue over her tender lips, she said huskily, 'He was saying goodbye.'

'He didn't kiss *me* goodbye,' Nick said, disgruntled. 'Where's my towel?'

'Behind you.' Kate forced herself to speak calmly, to go with him into the apartment, to behave normally, when all the time she felt as though Patric had branded her with that kiss.

It was over. They'd spent the morning shopping for clothes and presents—including a weather station Nick fell in love with and refused to be parted from—and now they were all packed and ready to go. Kate made one last round of the rooms, in case they'd overlooked anything, and after glancing at her watch checked for the third time that their passports were in the pocket in her bag. 'Come on, Nick, time to go.'

The hour-long trip up the motorway and across the huge bridge over the Brisbane River assumed a dream-like aspect. Kate answered Nick's questions, periodically looking above his head at the hot, sparse landscape outside; she organised them competently off the bus, and steered the luggage trolley across the wide terminal to check in, waiting while the clerk tapped information into her computer.

'Ah, you've both been upgraded,' she said, smiling, after a quick glance at their passports. 'You'll have a more comfortable ride back.'

'How's that?' Kate asked, frowning.

The clerk looked again at her computer screen. 'It happens,' she said lightly. 'The plane's not very full tonight so they've put some lucky people up. I'd just enjoy it if I were you.'

'We'll do that,' Kate said with a smile, accepting the boarding passes. 'Thank you.'

After watching their cases disappearing down the conveyer belt, Nick insisted on a complete tour of the light, airy, tree-shaded concourse.

For once Kate found his comments and observations tiring. Making herself relax, she tried to enter into his enthusiasm, and succeeded well enough until eventually they sat down in one of the cafés for a drink.

When Nick had half drained his glass, he said, 'Mr Sutherland lives in Auckland, doesn't he?'

'Yes.' Kate knew she sounded abrupt, so she smiled.

Nick poked his straw into the ice at the bottom of his glass. 'Will he come up to see us in Whangarei?'

You too? she thought painfully. 'I don't think he'll have time to do that, Nick.'

Nick prodded some more, his long lashes dark against his golden skin. He didn't look at her as he said in a gruff voice, 'Won't we ever see him again?'

'He's a very busy man,' Kate said gently. 'But you had a good time here, didn't you?'

'Yes.' He drew a complicated pattern on the surface of the water with his straw. 'I liked it better when Mr Sutherland was with us.'

Kate began to talk of school, of what Nick would be able to tell his classmates about his holiday, of the things Anna and Jacob next door would find particularly interesting, and with the swiftness of childhood Nick forgot that he was sad and began to enthuse again.

Listening to him remind himself of the thrill of one particular roller-coaster, Kate knew there'd be moments of wistfulness whenever he remembered Patric, although eventually even they would fade until he only recalled the pleasure.

It might even happen for her too.

Before long their flight number was called.

'Up the front,' the steward on the plane said, smiling

professionally as Kate showed him the boarding passes. 'On the right, madam.'

She walked up through the throngs of passengers, then stopped.

'May I help?' An attendant appeared from nowhere.

'I think I need to go further on,' Kate said, glancing at her pass, 'but this screen seems to tell me I shouldn't go through.'

The attendant examined the passes. 'Keep going,' she said.

Waiting by the screen was another attendant, dark-suited, as dignified as a head waiter.

'Ah, we were wondering where you were,' he said, smiling at Nick, who was looking about him with frank and obvious interest. 'This way.'

Here the seats were large, and to Nick's delight each had a small television screen mounted in the arm. Did ordinary travellers routinely get bumped up to first class?

'Here we are,' the steward said, stopping. 'Would you like to sit next to the window, sir?'

'My name's Nick,' Nick said gravely. 'Can I sit next to the window, Mummy?'

'May I,' she corrected. 'Yes, of course.'

'May I?' Nick repeated, scrambling into his seat with alacrity.

Just before she sat down she cast a glance around the rest of the section, but of course Patric's black head wasn't anywhere there. And in spite of the desk clerk's comment that the plane wasn't full, first class was.

This, she thought as she clipped the seatbelt around her, was how Patric travelled all the time. And of course he wouldn't have organised it—why should he?

She had no illusions; his kindness might indicate a streak of chivalry beneath the tough, hardened business-man façade, but once he'd discovered that Nick wasn't his son his pressing interest must have died. He'd kissed her because he was angry, but by now he'd probably put them out of his mind.

As the plane took off, and they were pampered all the way across the Tasman, Kate tried to convince herself that those days in Surfers' Paradise had provided her with some sort of closure, a feeling that all the ends had been tied up and she could now face the future unimpeded by baggage from the past.

Unfortunately her response to that kiss revealed a much more unpalatable truth. She was every bit as susceptible to Patric as she had been all those years ago. The golden glamour of his youth had been replaced by a potent male charisma, part intelligence, part dynamic power, part controlled determination. And beneath that smouldered an indefinable magnetism that called to her with a sensual promise against which she had no defence.

CHAPTER FIVE

THEY landed on an Auckland spring night—wet, of course, and chilly after the burgeoning warmth of sub-tropical Australia. Nick, who'd slept most of the way across, didn't take too kindly to being wakened. His normal sunny temperament in abeyance, he trailed alongside Kate, complaining while they waited for their luggage to emerge on the carousel.

'Darling, that's enough,' Kate finally said.

He gave her a belligerent glower. 'My eyes feel sticky.'

'It won't be long now. Just hang on in there.'

As she heaved their cases off the carousel and stacked them on the trolley Kate thought wryly that although it was politically incorrect to like being cared for, just occasionally it would be wonderful to have a strong-armed man to heft luggage about.

Of course they had to wait in the Immigration and Customs hall; two other planes had arrived just before them—one, she saw, a Sutherland Aviation jet, also from Brisbane. Patric would have been on it...

Ruthlessly wrenching her mind back from that dangerous path, she concentrated on shuffling towards the desks. Thankfully Nick had forgotten his crossness in the excitement of watching a little sniffer dog bustling around. Then at last they were through and walking into the Arrivals area.

Sally Pickering, with her shock of vivid red hair, should have stood out like a bonfire on a dark night. No doubt if she'd been there she would have.

'You can sit down here and look after our suitcases while I go to the desk and see if she's left a message,'

Kate said firmly, wheeling their trolley towards a bank of seats.

Nick's lip wobbled. 'Has she forgotten us?' he asked soberly.

'Not Sally. She'll have—'

'Mr Sutherland!' he exclaimed, his face lighting up. 'Look, there's Mr Sutherland! He'll find Sally for us!'

'Don't shout!' But Kate's heart clamoured in her breast.

She followed Nick's gaze and saw Patric striding across the concourse, accompanied by a man wearing the sort of clothes you'd choose to impress the boss late at night, and a woman in tailored trousers and a silk shirt, a jacket slung across one elegant, slim shoulder.

Patric swung around. His brows drew together and he turned back to speak to the other two, who stopped and waited as he headed purposefully towards Kate and Nick.

'Good flight?' he asked, as though he'd never kissed her.

'Great, thank you,' Kate returned in her briskest tone. 'We were upgraded to first class and had a wonderful time, didn't we, Nick?'

'Cool,' he agreed, gazing worshipfully at Patric, his tired face split by a smile.

Ignoring the intrigued and speculative stares from the two people who'd met Patric—and every woman within eyesight—Kate went on, 'We won't keep you, Patric. Thank you for making our last few days in Australia such fun.'

The arrogant mouth didn't soften. 'I had fun too,' he said negligently. 'Where's the friend who was going to meet you?'

Thwarted in her attempt to make a dignified and final goodbye, Kate admitted, 'She's not here yet. But she won't be long—she's very reliable, is Sally.'

Nick sagged against her, lost in an enormous yawn.

'How about her car?' Patric asked after a grim glance at the boy. 'Or is it like Eugene, prone to breakdowns?'

Kate put her hand on her son's shoulder, holding him steady. 'It's reliable too. She's just running a little late. And if she can't make it she'll have left a message for us.'

As though her words had summoned it, a pleasant female voice said over the intercom, 'Would Ms Brown— Ms Kate Brown—please come to the Information Desk.'

Patric said abruptly, 'Stay there, I'll go. Give me your passport.' When she stared at him, he said, 'I don't think they'll believe I'm Ms Kate Brown.'

Nick gave a crow of laughter, and Kate smiled but said, 'Patric, you've got people—'

'They'll wait,' he said, holding out his hand. 'I won't be a moment.'

The previous sleepless night must have clouded her brain, because she handed over the passport and watched him make his way through the press of people to the Information Desk. It might have been his height or those wide shoulders, but it was more probably the aura of dynamic power that had them parting before him like the waters before Moses. His casual clothes, although tailored to fit him, didn't mark him out from the other men there, but it was amazing how many eyes followed his progress.

Repressing a stark pang of isolation, Kate looped her arm around her son. Warm, lax, his eyes heavy with interrupted sleep, Nick gazed silently after his hero. More passengers emerged from the Arrivals Hall, were enveloped in greetings, and disappeared through the doors into the night.

The girl on the Information Desk cheered up when Patric arrived, bestowing on him a smile that went well beyond professional goodwill. He spoke; she nodded, then peered at Kate's passport and looked across. Kate gave a wave that indicated, she hoped, that she was Kate Brown.

With another dazzled smile the woman handed over an envelope. Kate braced herself. If Sally had been called away she and Nick would have to spend the rest of the night at the airport, because she didn't have enough money to pay for a motel. Every cent of holiday money was gone, and she wasn't going to hock herself to her credit card.

'She rang it in about three hours ago,' Patric told her as he handed the envelope over.

Kate's fingers shook as she slit it open. Sally's grandmother in Wellington had had a heart attack and wasn't expected to last the night, so Sally was driving down with her brother. She was so sorry... The hasty scrawl tailed off into an indecipherable signature.

Damn, Kate thought, why hadn't she left a key to her house?

And immediately she felt mean and selfish. Sally was devoted to her grandmother, and anyway, shuttles didn't go out as far as Albany.

Oh, well, a night at the airport wasn't going to mark her or Nick for life!

'What's happened?' Patric asked, as though he had the right to.

In her crispest, most confident voice she told him. He looked down at Nick, visibly drooping. 'What will you do?'

Kate said confidently, 'Nick and I will manage.'

Patric's eyes narrowed as he surveyed her face. In response Kate straightened her shoulders and tilted her chin.

Calmly he said, 'You can come home with me.' He cut off her instant rejection. 'What time do you catch your bus tomorrow morning?'

'It leaves Auckland at eight-thirty.' Tempted, she ploughed on, 'You're very kind, Patric, but of course we can't plonk ourselves onto you like this. I promise you I can deal with—'

'I'm sure you can,' he interrupted, impatience threading the words. 'But why bother when you don't need to? I live in an apartment block on the waterfront—all you'll need to do in the morning is take the lift down and walk just over a block to the bus depot.'

Nick gave a prodigious yawn.

'You and Nick can sleep in the guest bedroom,' Patric said deliberately, divining her reservation with an accuracy that sent heat licking across her skin.

'Can we, please?' Nick asked, his voice rough with exhaustion. 'May we, I mean?'

The decision was made by Patric, who took the handle of the luggage cart and headed into the press of people.

'Hey!' Kate exclaimed, scooping Nick along with her as she set off after Patric's arrogant figure. He stopped by the two people he'd abandoned. Interesting, Kate thought angrily, to see their instant attention.

Two heads nodded while he spoke with curt rapidity. As she and Nick came up to them he said, 'I'll see you at nine tomorrow morning. Goodnight.'

Again they nodded, smiled at Kate and Nick, made brief farewells and left.

'Patric,' Kate began, following him as he picked up his suitcase and settled it onto the trolley, then wheeled it through the doors.

She'd meant to tell him he was overbearing and autocratic, and insist on managing her own affairs, but when they stepped out into the cold darkness and she felt the rain on her face and Nick's hand suddenly cling to hers she admitted defeat.

As Patric had known she would, she thought crossly, already regretting it. But what harm could a night do?

Patric commandeered a taxi and put them into it, gave the driver the address and got in himself, helping Nick put on his seatbelt. Kate fumed, 'Talk about high-handed.'

'You were going to dither,' he said levelly. 'This is the most sensible way of dealing with the situation, and you know it.'

'I don't like being bulldozed.'

'No one does. Give it a rest, Kate—you can shout at me when we don't have an audience.'

Nick was sitting very quietly—too quietly. Shamefacedly Kate said, 'Ah, well, it's rather fun being in a taxi whizzing through Auckland in the middle of the night, isn't it, Nick?'

'Yes.' His voice was uncertain, but only five minutes into the trip he relaxed sideways onto Kate, abandoning himself again to sleep.

Tensely Kate cuddled him, waiting for Patric to speak. He was probably thinking he'd gone crazy, inviting two strays home for the night, she thought gloomily.

The taxi drove steadily through rain, long needles of it flashing towards the windscreen like darts until the taxi swung off the motorway into the streets of the inner city. Slowing, the taxi turned beneath a portico.

Welcome to spring, Kate thought as the engine died.

The holiday was over, yet she didn't feel depressed. In fact, excitement sizzled with delicate, feverish precision along her nerves. While Patric and the driver organised the luggage she got out of the vehicle and reached for Nick. He was sound asleep so she had to pick him up. She managed to get him into her arms, but staggered as she straightened up.

Patric looked up; some transient emotion glittered in the dark eyes. 'Give him to me,' he commanded, striding around the end of the cab.

Kate said, 'It's all right.'

'He's too heavy. Hand him over—you won't be able to carry him all the way up.'

Reluctantly she accepted his help, looking down into her son's blissfully unconscious face with a pang as she handed him over.

'What's the matter?' Patric asked, holding the boy easily.

'It's silly—but I've always been able to carry him before.'

'He's growing up.' The few conventional words sounded like a condemnation, but as he was striding away from her towards the door she might have misheard him.

Shivering in the raw air, Kate followed him.

When he stopped he said, 'The key card's in my right-hand jacket pocket. Get it out and unlock the door, will you?'

Carefully, Kate inserted her hand into his pocket and found the card. She put it into the lock, then did the same with an interior door. The taxi driver, a suitcase in each hand, followed them in.

A smooth, discreetly luxurious and very fast lift took them all up. Kate stood with her eyes averted from the man who held her son so carefully in his arms.

'The same key,' he said when the lift stopped to reveal just one door in a carpeted vestibule. 'My front door,' Patric told her. 'The light switch is inside on the left.'

Kate used the key card again, pushed the door open and turned on the lights. They revealed a hall, complete with mirror above a modern Italian-style console table in polished dark wood. An abstract painting in moody blues and golds smouldered against pale walls, and a superb plant stood in an elegant oriental pot.

'Your bedroom's the third door to the right,' Patric said. 'It doesn't look as though anything disturbs him.'

'No.' Lifting Nick's case, Kate walked slightly ahead so that she could push the door open and switch the lights on in the bedroom.

Lamps flowered in the ceiling and on either side of two large single beds. Patric laid Nick down on one of them, and stood for a moment looking down at the sleeping child, his expression guarded. Was he regretting that Nick wasn't his son? When he looked up and saw Kate watching him his mouth tightened.

'I'll pay the cab driver and bring in your luggage,' he said.

Chilled, Kate held out the key. 'Thank you.'

In spite of the warmth of the room she shivered again, oppressed by the ghosts of dead emotions. Brushing aside their inchoate warnings, she began to untie Nick's brand-new sneakers, his pride and joy.

She was easing his jeans down his legs when Patric spoke from the door. 'Does he always sleep so soundly?' he asked quietly, setting down Kate's suitcase.

'Usually. He's extra tired tonight, of course.'

Golden light from the bedside lamps gleamed on Patric's black head, picking out with loving intensity the stark planes and angles of his face, the slightly darker bronze of his five-o'clock shadow as he said, 'The beds are already made up. The bathroom is through that door— you'll find towels in the cupboard beside the hand basin. I'll go down and bring back my case.'

Nodding, Kate deftly removed Nick's shirt, rolled him over, pulled back the bedcover and inserted him between the sheets. He mumbled something but didn't stir, apart from hunching away from the light. Kate smoothed a lock of hair from his brow and kissed his cheek.

'Thank you,' she said to Patric, who had returned by then.

'Do you want a drink, or something to eat?'

She shook her head. 'No, thank you. I think I'll go straight to bed.'

'What time do you want to be woken?'

'I'll set my alarm for seven,' she said, turning to smile uncertainly at him. 'This is very kind of you, Patric.'

He stood like a sentinel in the doorway, the hard face formidable. 'Then goodnight, Kate,' he said, and although his voice was gentle there was a metallic light in the eyes that scrutinised her face.

She had to swallow, and even then her voice was croaky with strain. 'Goodnight, Patric,' she said.

When the door closed silently behind him her breath sighed out between her lips.

Kate looked at her son, still peacefully sleeping, and the old turmoil of regret and bitterness and love welled up. No, best not to think of it; she'd made her decisions and she'd stick with them.

Nick was nothing like his father. He would grow up

respecting women, liking them too much to believe that they were all whores at heart. And Patric had no place in their lives.

Grim-faced, Kate knelt by her suitcase, opened it and took out her sponge bag and T-shirt.

The bathroom that led off the bedroom was all marble, in soft creams and rosy pinks. How much had it cost? More than her entire income for a year, she thought cynically, but it was gloriously plush. After she'd worked out how the space-age controls functioned she had a splendid shower.

While drying herself she looked at her reflection in the huge mirror, wondering at first because the steam hadn't clouded it with moisture. How had they done that? No doubt it needed expensive equipment. It didn't seem worth it, just to look at yourself.

That wide expanse of fog-free glass seemed to epitomise the enormous difference between her and Patric. Coming here had been a mistake, as had letting Patric spend time with them in Australia. She'd made more than enough mistakes where he was concerned, and as she didn't seem able to learn from the past it was just as well she wouldn't be seeing him again.

But when she lay in the luxurious bed, more comfortable than any she'd ever slept in, and listened to the muted sounds of traffic and Nick's occasional little snuffle, she wondered whether forgetting him was going to be so easy.

Perhaps she should also consider the fact that a traitor was at work inside her—the adolescent passion that had never died.

Restlessly she turned over onto her back. Was Patric just through the wall? An unbidden tide of erotic anticipation swamped her as she pictured him, long and lean and tanned, sable hair on a white pillow, a lamp illuminating with excruciating accuracy the smooth olive skin, the long-boned arms and legs, the flat stomach and narrow male hips...

He'd always been beautiful to her, so strong and confident in his masculinity, so assured—to her and every other woman, she thought acidly, recalling the revealingly envious, unspoken accolades of other women.

The reason her fixation still existed was probably because she and Patric had only made love once before her blossoming sensuality had been shattered by the nightmare experience of rape and brutality.

Perhaps, her brain suddenly said, you should have an affair with him and get him out of your system.

Forget you ever thought that, Kate commanded, turning onto her side to woo sleep with desperate fervour.

She had almost made it when she snapped awake again, remembering the plastic bag with Nick's treasured weather station in it. Frowning, she tried to recall its arrival in the apartment.

It hadn't; she'd have remembered the distinctive bag Nick had carried onto the plane and insisted on having under his seat all the way across the Tasman. She recalled Patric handing it to Nick when they'd got into the back seat of the taxi; she hadn't thought of it when she'd picked him up.

He'd be desolate if it was lost.

Perhaps it had been left at the front entrance. Moving silently, she got up and slipped out of the bedroom, down the tiled hall, its warmth telling her there was underfloor heating. At the front door she switched on the light, but no plastic bag stood there.

'What's the matter?'

She whirled. Patric stood watching her, still fully clothed, although he'd changed. He now wore jeans and a cotton shirt. Paradoxically, he looked infinitely more unapproachable in them than he had before.

Feeling crucially underdressed in her T-shirt nightgown, Kate explained.

His frown deepened. 'I don't remember seeing it, and I didn't bring it in. I'll ring the taxi company.'

Although his eyes hadn't strayed from her face, she wanted to go back into the bedroom and close the door on him and hide. Which was stupid, because her nightgown covered her thighs and shoulders quite adequately. There was no reason to feel so exposed.

Yet even her bare feet felt vaguely provocative.

'Thank you, that's a good idea,' she said, trying to sound perfectly normal—as though they had never exchanged that last searing kiss.

Because it seemed rude not to, she followed him into what was clearly an office, a large room with a huge desk and some sophisticated computer equipment gleaming and humming and blinking at her.

'Were you working?' she asked blankly.

He picked up a telephone and dialled. 'Yes. Hello, I'm reporting something left in one of your cabs.'

Kate stood while he concisely told the operator what had happened. A huge rug kept her feet pleasantly warm.

'I see,' Patric said. 'Thank you. Yes, before eight o'clock.'

Alerted by a note in his voice, Kate looked up. He was watching her while he spoke, his eyes travelling in a leisurely inspection from her toes, buried in the rug, the length of her legs and on further, finally coming to rest on her face. Heat burned through her skin, but she held his gaze, refusing to be intimidated.

He didn't take his eyes off her while he put the receiver down. 'The cab driver has already handed it in,' he said conversationally. 'Someone will deliver it before eight tomorrow morning.'

'Thank you very much,' she gabbled, and turned to flee without thought for dignity.

'Kate?' He said her name as though it was a rare jewel, as though he treasured it, held it in his hand and warmed it with his lifeblood.

She froze. 'What?'

'Do you remember the night we made love?'

Her head jerked as though he'd hit her. 'Why?' she asked huskily.

'Have you forgotten, Kate?'

She dragged in a shuddering breath. 'No, I remember.'

He moved silently, but her skin warned her. When he lifted her hair from the back of her neck, threading his fingers through the silken tangle, sifting it, letting it fall back against her sensitive skin, the unbearable expectation made her flinch.

In a voice chilled by contempt, he said, 'It's all right, I'm not going to attack you.'

'I didn't think you were,' she said, realising that he'd misunderstood her reaction. 'I—I'm not used to this, that's all.'

After a moment of silence he stepped back. Bitingly he asked, 'Is this how you've lived since Nick's birth—like a coward, refusing every challenge, retreating into the tight little community of two you've made with your son? I'm surprised, Kate. I thought you had more guts.'

'No,' she said angrily, 'I have not lived like that!' She pivoted, her eyes dark and turbulent as she fought for control.

Patric smiled cynically. 'It's safe, I suppose—until Nick wants to leave home. What will happen then?'

Between her teeth she said, 'He'll go with my blessing.'

'I doubt it,' he said unforgivably. 'Not if he's the focus of your universe.' He sounded bored and indifferent. 'You look tired. Go back to bed, Kate.'

Furious and bewildered, her stomach churning, she walked out of his office and into her bedroom. He wanted her; she knew he wanted her. And if she could have taken easy, uncomplicated pleasure in his body she'd have gone to bed with him. But she couldn't.

While she'd stood there, made captive by his hard grey eyes, she'd been stormed by a discovery that shattered the brittle armour of her composure. Its shards splintered her soul, cutting away the past years, revealing her emotions in naked, shuddering urgency.

She'd been so sure of her independence, her autonomy; now she knew that somehow she was still tied to him by bonds that had never loosened. She might no longer love Patric, but she was acutely, primally aware of him with a cell-deep intensity.

Once she'd read that women never forget, never become entirely free of the men they lose their virginity to. She'd scoffed, but now she wondered whether some elemental linkage did shackle a woman to the man who'd initiated her into the pleasure of the senses.

'Mummy! Mummy, wake up! Mr Sutherland's here and he says you should get up!'

Kate lifted a reluctant eyelid and glared at her son. 'What?'

Patric's voice, smooth and amused, snapped her eyes wide open. 'You forgot to set your alarm. It's a quarter past seven, so if your bus leaves at eight-thirty you should probably get up now.'

'I'll be right out,' she mumbled, forcing the miasma of too little sleep too late from her brain.

'You're not running late yet. I'll give Nick some breakfast.'

She lifted her face an inch from the pillow. Nick had dressed himself in one of the new shirts and the jeans she'd bought, and judging by his wet forelock and virtuous smile he'd washed his face.

'Thank you,' she muttered.

At least she'd had the sense to stay prone, so Patric wouldn't see her with her hair all over her face and her eyes full of sleep. The instant the door closed behind them she leapt out of bed, thanking heaven that she wasn't one of those unfortunate people who found waking up seriously difficult.

Fifteen minutes later, showered and dressed, her armour

of composure buckled and fastened, she followed the sound of voices to find Patric and Nick in a sophisticated kitchen and family room.

Nick had seated himself at the table and was draining a glass of orange juice as Patric set a plate before him and said, 'See how you like that muesli.'

Although she sensed a taut impatience in the dark, penetrating eyes, he smiled at Kate as though nothing had happened in his office the previous night.

Nothing had. She didn't want any sort of relationship with Patric. It was too dangerous.

Acutely self-conscious, she bent to kiss Nick's forehead and said, 'He likes most mueslis.'

'But we make our own, with rolled oats and yoghurt and apples from our apple tree,' Nick said cheerfully, returning her kiss with a hug. 'I like that best. Mum, I s'pose our lettuces and cabbages are going to be ready now, do you think?'

Kate straightened. 'Yes, although I told the MacArthurs to use any that looked as though they should be eaten.'

He nodded and picked up his spoon while Patric asked, 'The MacArthurs are the parents of Nick's best friend?'

Did he ever forget anything? His level scrutiny made Kate very thankful she'd succumbed to vanity and worn her best pair of trousers and a shirt, both the smoky dark green that enhanced her green-blue eyes. Slipping into the chair he pulled out for her, she said, 'Yes, they're Rangi's parents.'

'I haven't got a real aunt, but Aunty Ngaire is my pretend one,' Nick said. 'Rangi's in my class at school—he's my best friend and my pretend cousin.'

'Rangi's the youngest of four brothers, so Ngaire's an old hand at parenting. She and Rangi steered us through play school and kindergarten,' Kate said prosaically, accepting a glass of juice from Patric. It was superb, freshly squeezed and tasty. 'Mmm, delectable,' she breathed after the first delicious, sweetly tart sip. 'I'll bet those oranges came from Kerikeri.'

'I have a friend with an orchard there who ships me down the occasional bag. What would you like to eat? I can cook you something—or there's porridge?'

He sounded just like a good host, so she endeavoured to be the perfect guest. 'It sounds wonderful, thank you, but I'll just have some toast. Don't get up—show me where the toaster is.'

But Patric got to his feet and put in a couple of slices from a loaf he'd clearly just got out of a freezer. 'Do you drink coffee at breakfast?'

'Yes, thank you.'

It was hot and invigorating—and better still, it gave her eyes and hands something to do while she waited for the toast.

Patric was eating porridge. As she glanced at it he lifted his dark brows at her. 'My Scottish grandmother firmly believed that if you didn't eat porridge you not only risked a life of moral turpitude—don't laugh, that's the word she used!—but you'd come to a bad end. She was a good propagandist. Although,' he added smoothly, 'I must confess I only eat it in cold weather.'

If he ate porridge, who did he keep the muesli for?

'It's supposed to be extremely good for you.' Kate knew she sounded stilted, but this was altogether too cosy.

She didn't trust her reactions to him, or to the occasion. It was too easy for such moments to become fodder for dreams.

And she was finished with dreams. Her life was a constant struggle with money, bringing up a child without a father, and the understanding that she wasn't likely to find herself with either a marriage or a particularly satisfying career. She'd done her best with the meagre hand fortune had dealt her, and she would continue to play it as well as she could, but she and Patric had nothing in common beyond a long-ago summer fling.

And on her side, at least, a violent physical attraction that didn't know when to die.

'Is porridge good for boys too?' Nick demanded. 'And what does t-turpitude mean?'

Kate smiled at him. 'Porridge is good for everyone, and turpitude means excessive badness.'

He looked at Patric's plate. 'I said no thank you because I didn't know what it tasted like.'

'Would you like to try some?' Patric asked.

Nick nodded, and Patric got up and disappeared into the kitchen. He came back with a small bowl containing a tiny amount of porridge, and the two slices of toast for Kate.

'Does it have sugar in it?' Nick asked, surveying the porridge.

Patric's brows lifted. 'Only Sassenachs eat their porridge with sugar,' he said austerely, in a passable Scots accent. 'Real people have it with salt.'

Nick grinned. 'What are Sass-Sassenachs?'

'Saxons. People who live in England.'

Nick picked up his spoon. Kate spread honey on her toast and tried to ignore the man serenely eating porridge across the table.

'It tastes good,' Nick said approvingly, and demolished the rest. 'We don't live in England, we're New Zealanders. So we're not Sassenachs, are we?'

'No,' Patric and Kate said together.

Nick looked puzzled. 'Why do they have it with sugar and we don't?'

Kate hid a smile, but Patric explained the millennia-long rivalry between Saxon and Celt with clarity and conciseness. Nick nodded, taking it all in.

And again an odd frisson of loneliness, of exclusion, shivered through Kate. It was ridiculous; it was also entirely natural. All Nick's life she'd been the only person he'd had to answer questions—and yet that wasn't true. He spent long hours with Jacob and the MacArthurs, and she'd never been jealous or felt left out.

Nick asked, 'Mummy, are we Scottish?'

'No. There's a little bit of Irish in us,' she said, 'But I'm afraid most of us is plain yeoman stock from England—people who ate bacon and eggs for breakfast, not porridge.'

Clearly his heart was set on Scottish ancestry, like his idol, because he demanded, 'What about my father? Was he Scottish?'

'I don't think so,' she said quietly. 'Finish your breakfast. We have to get ready soon.'

Nick gave her an exasperated look, but set to work on the rest of his food with his usual gusto, while Kate forced toast and coffee down, joining Patric in a civilised, meaningless conversation entirely suited to two strangers who just happened to be eating breakfast together, with the almost-six-year-old son of one of them listening.

When they'd finished she offered to do the dishes, but Patric shook his head. 'There's a dishwasher.'

She got to her feet, noting that he did the same. 'What about the beds? I'll strip them—'

'That's the housekeeper's job,' he said bluntly. 'Go and get ready. Oh, the lost luggage arrived early this morning. It's on the hall table. How did you sleep?'

'Very well, thank you,' she said, turning away to stack dishes on the bench.

He said, 'I didn't. I spent a lot of my time remembering that you were asleep a few feet away.'

Shortly after eight Patric knocked on the open bedroom door. 'I'll get the bags,' he said, and picked them up with effortless ease.

Kate and Nick followed him, but he put the bags down in the hall and said, 'You've got time to look at the view from the sitting room.'

Their bedroom had looked out over the city, with the Sky Tower dominating the view, but he led them into a huge room walled with glass overlooking the harbour.

From it a deck extended, furnished with pots and tubs of pansies and bamboo and other plants. Even on a cool spring morning with rain in the offing it looked lush and tropical. In summer, Kate thought, it must be magical.

Opening a door, Patric said to Nick, 'That's where the Whitbread yachts come in, and that, of course, is the harbour bridge you'll be going over shortly. Down there's the Maritime Museum, and if you look the other way that place with the funny little towers is the Ferry Building.'

Nick followed him fearlessly over to the balustrade. Kate stood just outside the door, gazing out over the glittering panorama. Nick would get over this affection for the man he'd known such a short time. She'd have to make sure he had plenty to do, plenty to think about, for the next few weeks.

'All right?' Patric asked, frowning, his dark eyes scanning her face. 'I'd forgotten you were afraid of heights.'

'I'm not afraid where there's a balustrade,' she said quickly.

He held out his hand. 'Then come on out.'

Kate looked up sharply. He'd used to scorn those who took dares, but there had been a challenging note in his voice that fired her. Ignoring his hand, she said, 'I don't need help, thanks,' and walked past him to join Nick, who was staring at a strange craft in the basin.

'Mum, that's Xena the Warrior Princess's boat,' he told her in awestruck tones. 'On television.'

Although they didn't own a television set, Kate knew that the popular series was shot in New Zealand. 'Is it?'

'Yes.' He stared reverently at the strange-looking craft. 'When I stayed with Rangi we watched that programme. It's a Greek boat. Xena's a Greek warrior princess.'

It was easy to see, Kate thought with a clutch of wry amusement, that the boat's presence in the Viaduct Basin only increased Patric's desirability as a human being.

Nick twisted to look up at his host. 'Have you seen it sailing?' he asked.

'Several times,' Patric told him, and grinned down at Nick's impressed face. 'It looks very strange. Come on, we can't stay out here—your bus will be waiting for you.'

He took them in his car on his way to work, and because he double-parked to let them off there was no time for awkward farewells, although he insisted on carrying the bags in and up to the counter.

Kate gave him her hand and said, 'Thank you, Patric.'

'My pleasure,' he said, and lifted her hand to kiss the palm.

Her heart flipped as he released her and turned to the boy he'd thought to be his son.

Nick held out his hand, and Patric shook it with gravity and a smile. 'Take care of your mother,' he said.

Nodding, Nick blinked and fought back tears. And Patric, thank heavens, ruffled the boy's hair, and turned and strode away.

CHAPTER SIX

JUST over two weeks later Kate had to stay late at work, so she arranged with Jacob and Anna next door to collect Nick from school. As she got out of the Mini he came bursting through their front door, followed by a grave Jacob.

Radiant-faced, he shouted, 'Mr Sutherland is in Disneyland in California in America, and he's written to me. It's a postcard. Look!'

He thrust a brightly coloured picture of a pirate ship into her hands. Turning it over, Kate stared down at the bold black printing.

Patric had addressed it correctly.

Dear Nick,

I went here with friends yesterday. It rained, but we had a good time. I thought of you when we saw the rides.

Yours, Patric Sutherland.

'Who is this man?' Jacob asked a little abruptly when Nick had scooted inside to collect his school bag.

'An old friend of mine,' Kate said, her smile trembling on her lips.

He gave her a shrewd look from beneath white brows. 'Who wishes to be a new friend? Or perhaps more than a friend? Anna smells a romance.'

His wife could be heard inside, fussing over Nick. Kate summoned a determined smile. 'No. He likes Nick, and feels a little sorry for him, I think.'

98

'So he is kind. Nicholas said that you had seen quite a bit of him in Australia. And that you stayed at his apartment in Auckland when you came back home.'

Kate managed to laugh. 'I hope Nick also told you that he and I slept in the same room!'

'It is none of my business,' Jacob said severely. 'But Nicholas is beginning to realise that most of his friends have fathers and he wonders why he should not. Also, you need someone to take care of you.'

Kate reached up and kissed him on the cheek. 'This is the end of the century, Jacob. Women take care of themselves now.'

'Perhaps,' he said, shaking his head over the vagaries of modern life, 'But it does not seem right. You are a young, beautiful, intelligent woman, and you would make some fortunate man very happy. You deserve a man who will make you happy too. And everyone needs someone to rely on. Even I rely on my Anna! Oh, well, one will come your way one day. Just make sure you choose a good man, who loves my small friend as well as his mother.'

'Believe me,' Kate said with quiet, complete sincerity, 'that would be the most important qualification.'

'Well, not *the* most important, perhaps,' Jacob returned drily, turning as Nick came bounding towards them, closely followed by Anna. 'Off you go.'

After Nick had put his school gear away, and Kate had changed and grabbed herself a cup of tea accompanied by a quick flick through the newspaper, she began preparing dinner.

'I'll have to write to Mr Sutherland,' Nick said, putting his lunchbox on the bench.

'You don't need to answer postcards.' Suddenly angry with Patric, Kate flicked open a broad bean pod with unnecessary vigour and extracted the plump green beans.

Nick's jaw firmed. 'You always make me write to people when they send me presents,' he said. 'I should thank him for his card.'

Like children the world over, Nick had to be vigorously coaxed into writing thank-you letters. If she ignored this he'd never get around to it. So she evaded the issue by asking, 'Will you take it to school and show the class?'

'Yes.' Then he frowned. 'No,' he said after a moment's thought. 'He's my secret. Do you want me to read my book to you?'

'Yes, please.'

Settling himself on a stool on the dinette side of the narrow breakfast bar, he began to read. As she peeled potatoes and scrubbed and sliced the vegetables for chicken stir-fry, Kate thanked heaven that he'd been born a reader. He thoroughly enjoyed the occasional television programme he watched with Rangi, but he didn't seem to miss it at all.

She couldn't remember seeing any sign of a set in Patric's opulent, beautifully decorated apartment. A wall of bookshelves, yes, but nothing electronic.

Probably he had a complete room dedicated to home entertainment, she thought cynically, slicing the meat into thin strips; a room decorated in the same clever, relaxed style as the sitting room to show off state-of-the-art equipment.

Kate piled the broad beans into a small saucepan and wondered why Nick's decision not to take that postcard to school had set off alarm bells. If Patric intended to continue sending him postcards, and if they unsettled him at all, she'd soon put a stop to it.

On Saturday mornings Nick played rugby. Because Kate almost always watched him, she often collected several children whose parents couldn't make it. The following weekend, however, the game was on a field close by, so she and Nick walked there.

A benign sun shone down onto a sodden world; it would have been more sensible to stay at home and make sure the week's used clothes went through her old washing ma-

chine instead of standing on the sideline of a muddy field
watching a pack of small boys scamper up and down with
such scant disregard for the rules that periodically she had
to stop herself from laughing.

Then Nick got the ball. Grinning, he headed for the line.
Unfortunately it was the wrong line.

Kate, along with the coach and half a dozen other desperate parents, yelled, 'Go back, Nick, run the other way.'

Miraculously he heard them, and slowed, looked around,
and realised his mistake. Forehead furrowed with concentration, he ran back through the other small boys, bewil-
dering so many of the opposition that he was able to fling
himself triumphantly into the mud at the correct end.

'Well done, Nick,' the coach roared. 'All right, you
boys, get back to the halfway line. Turn around now, turn
around.'

Laughing, Kate clapped. The woman standing next to
her said, 'Oh, they're gorgeous, aren't they? Is this his first
try?'

'His very first,' Kate said, inflated with pride.

'It won't be his last,' her companion prophesied sagely.
'That's my fifth son playing in the other team. Believe me,
I know junior rugby. He's got good instincts, your boy,
and he can run.'

She looked over Kate's shoulder and made a soft growl-
ing noise in her throat. 'Your husband?' she asked beneath
her breath. 'Lucky you!'

Startled, Kate turned. Iron-grey eyes met her gaze with
cool, compelling self-possession.

'Patric,' she said foolishly. 'What—what are you doing
here?'

'Watching Nick score a try,' he said, smiling at the
woman beside her.

It was effortless, that naked, formidable charm; Kate
watched with wry comprehension as her companion succumbed without a struggle.

'Hi,' she said, dimpling. 'Your son's playing very well—in fact, he's a natural.'

From further down the line someone yelled, 'Marie!' and she grinned.

'Better go. See you.'

Beating back an incandescent flare of joy, Kate waited until they were alone before asking tersely, 'How did you find us?'

'Your next-door neighbour told me where you'd be.'

'Jacob?' Somehow she had to control this violent delight, this stunned, shivering pleasure.

'Yes.' He was watching the little boys scatter and clump across the field. 'I gather they don't tackle or scrum.'

'No, they just tag each other,' Kate told him, her brain at last beginning to work. She tried to smile naturally, to sound normal. 'I'd rather hoped he'd play soccer, but Nick's had his heart set on rugby ever since he watched Rangi's older brothers play.'

'You didn't try to change his mind?'

'Of course I did, but it was hopeless, so I gave up. I save my strength for the really important issues.'

Patric grinned. 'For a moment I thought he was going to score for the opposition.'

'That happens reasonably often, although the spectators usually manage to yell loudly enough to stop it.' Happiness unfurled on slow, heavily beating wings.

She had, she thought despairingly, waited almost seven years for this—had never stopped waiting. Oh, she'd got on with her life, but immured behind barred and locked doors in her heart—ignored, quiescent, yet expectant—had been the Kate who'd fallen in love with Patric when she was sixteen and never been able to fall out of it.

That Kate had never given up hope.

And that hidden Kate—innocent, ardent, trusting, impractical—was a real threat to the secure life she'd built so painfully.

Why hadn't Patric bowed out gracefully? That moment

of charged desire in his office had revealed that he wanted her, but was he wracked by the same powerful hunger for completion?

Or did he plan an affair? It had to be wishful thinking to hope that they might be able to breach the barrier of the disillusioned years and build something true and lasting from the debris.

Because that sort of ending only came in fairy stories, she told herself with brusque common sense. Patric was one of the richest men in New Zealand—in the Pacific Basin! He owned and headed a worldwide force in aviation. What did they have in common beyond the memory of an enchanted love affair when they had both been young enough to believe that miracles could happen?

She didn't dare risk her peace of mind. Or Nick's.

After watching in silence for some minutes, the man beside her commented, 'He has good hands for a six-year-old.'

'Some might think ''he has good hands'' to be pretty lukewarm praise for a player as brilliant as Nick.'

Patric laughed. 'I refuse to believe you're a foolishly doting mother.'

'Doting, certainly. Foolish—no, I hope not.'

'You've made a good job of him. He's a great kid.'

'He's happy,' she said, and gathered her strength around her like armour. 'Patric, I don't think it would be wise for you to keep up this...friendship.'

The expression on his tough face didn't alter, yet she knew her blunt statement had made him coldly, implacably angry. The Patric she'd loved had been self-controlled, but nothing like this.

Her chin lifted. She met his icy stare with courage, not backing down.

'Why?' he asked quite gently.

'Because he's happy the way things are. He doesn't need any grief in his life.'

'How will I make him unhappy?'

She was floundering, but she couldn't let him see it—he was too adept at mercilessly homing in onto weakness. 'You unsettle him,' she said, and even to her own ears it sounded lame.

'Why?'

Stiffening her already aching shoulders, she said quietly, 'He might grow to love you as the father he's never had, and I don't want his heart broken. It will be better if you don't see him or write to him.' She paused, then said deliberately, 'You have no claim to him, Patric. Accept it.'

His face hardened, and for a moment something implacable glittered in the gunmetal grey eyes. It vanished almost immediately, but it left her shaken. 'Are you threatening me?' he asked silkily.

'What with?' she asked, forcing an ironic note into the words. 'A scolding?'

'You can do better than that.' His narrowed eyes moved from her face to the swarm of boys. Without any inflection, he went on, 'As it happens, I was working on the assumption that one of the easiest ways to a doting mother's heart is through the object of that devotion. Which makes it very fortunate that I like the boy.'

Kate thought she'd misheard him. She stared at the autocratic profile while fragments of thoughts jostled for room.

Patric turned to look at her. 'Surprised?' he asked softly. 'Why, Kate? I never could leave you alone. You were like a siren, singing a song that stripped me bare of everything but the need to follow you. Hadn't you realised that it's still as strong as it ever was?'

A feverish heat clouded her mind. 'No,' she said warily. 'No, I hadn't. Realised, I mean.'

'I've had years to perfect the mask—I'm glad it works so well,' Patric said, a sardonic smile curving the long mouth. 'When you turned me down so conclusively at Tatamoa I couldn't believe that the most transcendental experience of my life had meant so little to you.'

His words stabbed her to the heart. Perhaps if she'd told him then what had happened—but she'd been shattered by the cruel ugliness of her experience. Appalled at the prospect of bearing her attacker's child and horrified by his threats, she'd been unable to face what had happened to her.

But Patric knew now. He knew, and he still wanted her.

Hard on the heels of that thought came another. Did she have the right to take the risk of falling in love again when she had Nick's well-being to consider?

Kate fixed her gaze on the ragged stream of small mud-encrusted boys as they formed into some kind of order. It took all of her determination to say, 'I'm not in the market for an affair. It would be bad for Nick—he's not accustomed to a series of temporary fathers.'

Thick black lashes drooped, half hiding Patric's eyes. She had a sense of that quick, controlled brain selecting and discarding options. After a moment he said, 'I wasn't suggesting an affair. I was thinking no further than the two of us getting to know each other again.'

Embarrassed by her mistake, she tucked a strand of hair into her beret. 'Patric—'

'I don't want any promises from you, any commitment, but you have my word that I do not treat this lightly.'

Kate turned her head away in case he should see her sudden hope. Looking blindly out onto the field, she heard the coach call something, and everyone clapped. Nick looked around, beamed when he saw her—or was it when he saw Patric?—and headed off towards the goalposts at the other end of the field.

'Kate,' Patric said unhurriedly, 'I swear to you that I've learnt a little in the past seven years—I won't abandon you again.'

'You didn't abandon me,' she protested. 'I broke it off.'

'Of course I abandoned you. As well as breaking my heart you shattered my pride, and I found it very hard to forgive you for that.' His voice was clipped, but she sensed the dark emotions curbed by his will. 'Kate, could we try again?'

The stark sincerity in his words undermined her defences. Temptation wove its glittering, seductive web around her, clinging in suffocating folds so that she couldn't think. Memories of that summer seduction—so beautiful, so precious to her—held her captive, but she had to leave them where they belonged, in the past. When she'd held Nick after his birth she'd made a promise that she'd always put his welfare above her own.

She hadn't realised the first real test of that vow would be so difficult to meet.

Tentatively she said, 'We could try, I suppose.' And was assailed by an eerie inevitability, as though this was somehow fated.

'You won't regret it,' Patric said with compelling determination, 'And neither will Nick.'

Dimly she heard the sound of a whistle, followed by both teams chanting the ritual of three cheers for each other and three for the referee. Then Nick came pounding across on muddy bare feet, his face lit with delight beneath the smears.

'Hello, Mr Sutherland,' he shouted, high on adrenalin and glory. 'Did you see my try? I was going to score at the wrong end, but I heard Mummy and I turned around and came back and I scored a try!'

Noisy, uninhibited, he vibrated with joy. Patric congratulated him, and any chance of changing her mind was gone; for better or worse she'd allowed the decision to be ratified.

When Patric suggested they drive home in his car she said, 'Nick's covered in mud. We'll walk back.'

'It's just a car,' Patric told her. Steady, thoughtful, uncompromising, his eyes held hers.

She looked at the sleek dark grey monster and prevented herself from shrugging. 'Well, if you're sure you don't mind.'

'I don't mind,' he said evenly.

Once in, he checked to make sure she and Nick both had their seatbelts on, then set the car in motion. Grinning, Nick waved to a group of his friends.

From the road her flat looked small and slightly grubby; with a very straight back and rigid shoulders Kate led them up to the front door and opened it. Cool, damp air greeted them; the sun had gone in, and without its warmth the rooms felt dull and chilly.

I am not ashamed of it, she thought defiantly. Aloud she said, 'Nick, into the bath, and make sure those knees and feet get a good scrub. Patric, which would you prefer, coffee or tea?'

'Tea, thank you,' he said promptly as Nick disappeared. 'Would you like me to make it?' He met her raised brows with a faint smile. 'I thought you might need to run the bath, or find clothes.'

Her answering smile was brittle. 'Nick is perfectly capable of running his own bath and finding his own clothes,' she said. 'Did you have a nanny when you were a child?'

Sometimes when Nick frowned she thought his brows twitched together like Patric's—the same wishful thinking that had led to her giving her son Patrick as a second name.

She was no longer in thrall to it; Patric was not Nick's father.

The past was over and done with, and this was the present—at once scary and exciting, offering a chance of happiness if only she was brave enough to reach for it.

'I had a nanny until I went away to school,' Patric said, his frown smoothing away as he watched her move around the small kitchen.

'How old were you when that happened?'

'Seven.'

She didn't say anything, but he must have recognised her outrage. 'My parents travelled a lot,' he explained.

'And although I missed them, and the nanny, I enjoyed boarding school.'

'Did you take your teddy with you?' she demanded.

He laughed. 'Yes. We all took our toys. And no, I don't believe it is as good a solution as living with a loving family. My children will stay at home, and I'll only travel when it's absolutely necessary.'

Was he trying to tell her something? No, she wouldn't head down that path, searching every throwaway comment for a hidden meaning. To the sound of the water running in the bathroom, she said, 'Children need their parents.'

And immediately wondered whether her remark amounted to an admission that Nick might be missing a father figure in his life.

Well, Patric wouldn't have time to fulfil that function. He'd be too busy to come up to Whangarei much.

Which, she thought sturdily as she measured tea into the teapot, was a good thing. A new beginning was all very well, but what exactly did he mean by it? Ruthlessly subduing the anticipation that bubbled up from some secret wellspring, she poured boiling water into the pot.

'Children do, indeed, need parents,' he said, an equivocal note in his voice sending a cold finger down Kate's spine.

Surely—no, he *knew* Nick wasn't his son!

He finished smoothly, 'Or good substitutes. You said you decided to keep Nick because you'd felt like an outsider in your family—I hadn't realised you were unhappy with your aunt and uncle.'

'I wasn't unhappy,' Kate said, lifting down two mugs and a glass, 'And it wasn't their fault that I never felt entirely at home. It could have happened in any family— there's often an odd one out.'

'An odd one out who's sure of her place, nevertheless,' he said shrewdly. 'You always looked like a gazelle in a herd of cows. They were good-looking and kind, but you were exquisite, a little fey, mysterious. I'm not surprised you felt different.'

Her heart thudded. 'They were *not* like cows, and they did their best. I'm very fond of them—we keep in close touch.'

The bath water stopped running. Kate groaned inwardly at the sound of an exuberant splash. Nick was excited, so there'd be water all over the walls and floor. Lifting her voice she said in a certain tone of voice, 'Nick, stop that!'

'OK,' he shouted, not in the least intimidated.

When he reappeared—hastily scrubbed and dressed—she and Patric had moved to the small sitting room that formed an 'L' with the dining alcove and kitchen. Kate watched her son carefully skirt a pile of library books and her heart cramped. He'd taken great pains—combing his hair back and putting on the jeans and surfing sweatshirt she'd bought him on their last day in Australia. A whiff of peppermint revealed that he'd even cleaned his teeth again.

All in Patric's honour.

'Any bruises?' she asked, making a place for him beside her on the elderly, barely comfortable suite she'd bought at a garage sale.

'A graze on my knee,' he said cheerfully. 'But it's all right; I put some sticking plaster on it.' He gave Patric a suddenly shy smile. 'I haven't got a try before,' he confided. 'That was my very first one.'

Patric said, 'It was an excellent try.'

'Did you play rugby when you were as old as me?'

Patric nodded. 'I was a forward,' he said, 'probably because I wasn't as fast as you are.'

Kate gave Nick his glass of water, and a cracker with cheese, and gradually relaxed her tense muscles as they discussed football. Patric's long legs seemed to stretch out over most of the floor; he dominated the small room, its shabbiness enlivened only by the sprigs of daphne she'd picked the previous day. Scent from the starry pink flowers floated—fresh, citrus-sharp yet sweet, the perfume of spring—on the cool air.

This was her home. She and Nick were comfortable and happy here.

The emotion that gnawed at her composure was neither dissatisfaction nor its sullen sibling, envy. No, she was worried and wary and edgy. And beneath those eminently sensible responses, slowly gathering strength, lurked a caged hunger. She recognised it, knew it well; she'd thought it long dead, but it had only needed Patric's presence to bring it back to life.

Now, looking around at the hard-won fruits of her recovery, she listened to Nick and Patric talk to each other. If she learned to love again—and if her love was rebuffed—would she cope?

Oh, yes, she'd cope. She'd found the strength to endure everything that had come her way so far. But why ask for trouble? Although she accepted his version of the events of seven years ago, this Patric Sutherland was a much tougher proposition than the golden man she'd fallen in love with.

Nick's voice—eager, thrilled—broke into her reverie. 'We could go to one of the places to eat down on the wharf,' he suggested. 'You know, Mummy, the ones we saw when we looked at the blue-water boats.' He turned back to Patric. 'Mummy liked the one from Seattle in America, but I saw one from Hamburg in Germany! All the way across the world! I liked it best.'

Patric's gaze met Kate's, his dark eyes limpidly amused. 'I thought you might like to go out to lunch.'

It was her last chance to say no, to send him out of their lives. She looked from his face to Nick's, and knew that she could not. If she ran away again, she would never forgive herself. 'That will be great,' she said, trying to hide the panicky edge in her voice. 'I'd better change into something a little more upmarket.'

Patric's dark glance slid to assess her clothes. Kate knew

that her favourite sage-green jersey enhanced the green in her eyes, and that the jeans, although old, were good quality and fitted well. Patric's expression didn't alter, but she felt his regard like a caress, and to her alarm her nipples tightened and flowered beneath the soft material of her bra.

'You look lovely just as you are,' he said quietly. 'Come on.'

Nick looked from one to the other, his brows furrowed, then asked loudly, 'Do you want me to change my clothes, Mummy?'

'No, you've already got your best clothes on,' she said, getting to her feet.

Following suit, Patric said drily, 'The possessive male.'

Standing very close to his mother, Nick asked, 'What's that?'

'You are,' Patric said, and smiled at him.

It had the usual effect. Nick returned the smile, and when Patric stood back to let Kate go ahead Nick did too. It wrung her heart. If Patric put a foot wrong this time he wouldn't have a shattered teenager to deal with; he'd have a furious mother!

Then Patric said, 'Give your mother room, Nick,' and after a moment Nick walked in front, looking over his shoulder while Patric took the key from her and locked the door.

Going down the path towards the car, she thought worriedly that Nick and she had been alone for so long that the addition of another person in their tight little twosome would mean a massive shift in the way they related to each other.

CHAPTER SEVEN

'I'M NOT surprised you come here—I remember how you loved the water,' Patric said, looking around him as they walked from the car park towards the town basin. 'This is all new, isn't it?'

'Yes. Have you been to Whangarei much?' It hurt that he should have visited the city and she hadn't known.

'I come here occasionally on business,' he said indifferently, still looking around. 'They've made a good job of it.'

Indeed the town basin, with its walks and plantings, its shops and busy restaurants, its fish and clock museums, was a thriving, bustling place.

'Mummy likes the boats,' Nick said, stopping to look down at one splendid white sloop, graceful as a heron in flight.

They always made Kate feel trapped, those yachts—big and beautiful with sleek lines, breathing adventure and freedom on wide waters. But life was a ledger of choices, opportunities taken or rejected. When she'd made the decision to keep Nick she'd accepted that she'd be giving up a lot for him; she didn't regret it.

'Yes,' Patric said quietly, and for a moment an unspoken communication flashed between them. He understood the longing for freedom, and the bonds of responsibility and love that tied her.

'I'm hungry,' Nick informed them, trying to sound pathetic.

'Then we'll go to that café,' Kate said. 'And as the sun's out and there's no wind we could sit outside.'

Struck again by a chill of alienation, Kate walked across

the sunlit pavement beside Patric, Nick running ahead. She had plenty of friends, and so did Nick, but when she thought of her life it seemed that she'd spent the past seven years lost in a fog of loneliness.

Patric had exposed her to the sun, and she was afraid of that bright light—of what it might reveal about her, of the effect it could have on her pleasant, humdrum life.

'What would you like to eat?' he asked, after he'd held out a chair for her.

She had no appetite. 'A sandwich,' she said quickly, scanning the blackboard menu. 'Tomato and cheese, or something like that. And a cup of coffee, please.'

'Nick?'

Nick said, 'Can we go inside and see what there is?'

'Of course,' Patric said. 'Do you want to come, Kate?'

'No, I'll sit here.' Her voice sounded odd—thin and distant, as though all emotion and spirit had been leached from her.

After another unsettling, too perceptive glance, Patric went inside with Nick. The sun umbrellas were furled, but the sky was now bright enough to make sitting out uncomfortable. Kate stood up and opened the one above their table, then sat down again and stared gravely across the paving, across the soft, sword-shaped leaves of the rengarenga lilies and their spikes of starry white flowers, across the masts and booms and graceful hulls of the yachts, across the busy road on the other side of the basin to the peaceful, bush-clad slopes of Parahaki beyond. Deliberately she let her mind go blank.

'You look *triste*,' Patric said.

Kate jumped. Clearly delighted with his world, Nick grinned at her, but Patric's face had set in lines of aloofness.

'I was thinking,' she said lamely.

Smiling narrowly, he said, 'I used to wonder what thoughts hid behind that haunting face. You were such a graceful, laughing thing, yet it was impossible to tell what you were feeling. You're more beautiful now, although you don't laugh nearly so much. What hasn't changed is the secrets hiding in those blue-green eyes.' He looked at Nick, busily draining a glass of water with a slice of lemon in it. 'Unlike this one,' he said obliquely. 'There's no wistfulness there.'

'He's a Scorpio, with all that that implies. And I'm not *wistful*, surely? It sounds weak and wishy-washy.'

'The wrong word,' he agreed. 'There's nothing weak about you. You might look vulnerable, but you're as strong as spun steel.'

He was wooing her with his deep, sensuous voice, with hypnotic dark eyes. Kate had to swallow before she could answer, 'I hope so.'

'I used to think you were made for journeys, as though you'd come from fairyland. And not the fairyland of little beings with gauzy wings either—you have a focused, dangerous intensity that's a warning as much as a lure.'

Sensation scudded the length of her spine, pulled her skin tight. Grabbing for an anchor of reality, she said, 'I was a silly adolescent, a nobody. And don't tell me your mother didn't point that out to you.'

'My mother comes from a culture with a rigid class system, and my father had old-fashioned ideas, although he never forgot that he'd come from farming stock.' His tone hardened. '*I* wasn't a snob.'

'No, you weren't,' she admitted.

'But?' A moment's silence until he said softly, 'Did they get to you, Kate?'

Damn the man, why didn't he let things ride?

Kate looked across at Nick, wholly concentrated on tackling a large piece of quiche. 'I don't entirely blame your parents for their feelings,' she evaded. 'It's foolish to pretend there are no social barriers in New Zealand.'

'There were—are—none between you and me,' he said curtly, and waited. When she didn't answer, he asked with latent, unspoken menace, 'What did they say, Kate?'

'Your mother was worried. She said that we—weren't suited,' she said, and gave a mirthless smile. 'I already knew that.'

He too was constrained by Nick's presence; Kate saw him reimpose control. 'She was wrong,' he said levelly. 'And so are you. It's still there, Kate—that provocative lure, the exquisite siren's song we both hear when we're together.'

Kate's brows climbed—hiding, she hoped, the sudden wild thud of her pulses. 'You're a romantic,' she said, forcing a light note into her voice. 'I wish I'd known that.'

Patric's smile was enigmatic. 'It's just as well you didn't,' he said. 'You played havoc enough with my life.'

Without missing a beat he initiated the sort of catching-up conversation that happens after many years apart. 'So your cousins are all married now?'

'And with children.' Kate had no appetite, but she took a small bite of the sandwich. 'Juliet and her husband are the closest—they own an orchard in Kerikeri.'

Patric nodded. 'My Aunt Barbara—Sean's mother—has shares in an orchard in Kerikeri. She really wanted to buy an ostrich farm, but I managed to persuade her it wasn't necessarily a brilliant investment.'

Which sounded as though Patric might now be in charge of the trust fund 'Black' Pat had set up for his daughter— or what was left of it after her husband, a good-looking weakling, had frittered away much of it by making one disastrous financial decision after another.

Kate looked at Nick and said, 'Darling, have you had enough?'

'There was a cake in there,' he said, hopefully eyeing Patric as the better bet.

Patric laughed. 'You'd better ask your mother.'

Kate would have agreed to anything that made Patric laugh. She'd loved his laugh, and she hadn't heard much of it since they'd met again. 'Of course you may have a cake,' she said. 'It's a special day—you did get a try.'

Her son's eyes gleamed. 'Can I—*may* I—have a cake every time I score a try?'

'Not every try. If you score ten tries in one game you don't get ten cakes,' she said, wondering what she'd started. Nick wasn't fiercely competitive, but when he'd made up his mind to do something he got there. Would he now score several tries every Saturday?

'Relax,' Patric said lazily, reading her mind, 'The rugby season must finish soon.'

'In a couple of weeks.'

Only when they'd disappeared inside the café did Kate close her eyes and release the breath pent in her lungs. Sean's name on Patric's lips was sacrilege.

She endured the waves of rage and pain and angry humiliation, let them wash over her without resistance, and eventually they ebbed, receded into the past. What had Sean done that had finally cut the family ties? She didn't care, provided they stayed cut.

But would Patric look at Nick differently if he knew that the boy was Sean's son?

Probably. Patric had despised his cousin, a handsome, malicious bully. And although Sean was all bluster, he'd been afraid of his younger cousin.

Halfway through that last holiday at Tatamoa he'd backed Kate into a corner at a party and tried to kiss her. Revolted and furious, she'd hit him in the solar plexus. He'd been doubled up and gasping when Patric had found them and spun him away with murder in his eyes, in his lethal voice. His excoriating summary of Sean's character, morals and behaviour had reduced his cousin to humiliated sullenness.

Years later, she'd decided that one of the reasons Sean had attacked her had been to salvage some mean remnant of pride.

Hearing his name still made her shudder, but she didn't care about him now—except for Nick's sake. However, if no one in the Sutherland family communicated with Sean, he'd never find out he had a son. Nick would be safe.

Kate's fingers tightened in her lap. A gull feathered its wings and swooped slowly over the basin, glinting silver in the spring sunlight, alien, solitary. So many decisions made in unbearable emotion—who was to say whether they'd been wrong or right? She'd done the best she could at the time, and had to live with the results.

Nick arrived back, carrying a plate with a slice of cheesecake complete with cream and dark blueberries. Beaming at his mother, he set it carefully down. 'Mr Sutherland says we can go to the playground in the park afterwards, if you want to,' he announced, and watched her closely.

'Of course I want to.' Her mouth curled into a stiff smile.

He nodded in a lordly fashion and proceeded to demolish the cheesecake. Kate flicked a glance at Patric, flushing at the sudden, savage heat that flamed within his eyes.

'How long are you going to keep me on a leash?' he asked, in an almost soundless voice.

Once again she endured a dislocating awareness. Every sense burst into action so that she drank in his colours and textures—the symmetry of bronze skin and blue-black hair, the arrogant line of his nose and chin, the beautifully chiselled mouth, the lithe, male grace that had prowled through so many dreams, so many fantasies down the years.

It wasn't just Patric she was attuned to, either, for Nick seemed to shimmer in his own radiance. Bewildered, Kate felt herself respond acutely, heart-shakingly, to the scents of coffee and salty water and growing things, to the passionate caress of the sun on her skin, to the taste of a wildfire hunger in her mouth.

Although a heavy weight seemed to have taken up residence just under her heart, a consuming, elemental tide of

awareness heightened every sense—the very air sparkled
and swept across her skin in a charged current.

Lust, she thought flatly. You're in lust again.

Unfortunately it wasn't plain, straightforward, uncomplicated desire. Sean's callous attack had ripped through
her life with the brutal efficiency of a chainsaw, its trauma
setting a barrier between her and the rest of the world. In
spite of her own hard work and the best efforts of her
counsellor, it was a barrier she'd never managed to overcome. She'd spent all those years hiding and not even
known it.

And now she wanted Patric again, yet she had no idea
how she would react if he touched her with true passion.
His kiss had sent her soaring, but would other, more intense responses be tainted by that act of violence?

Heat flowed inside her, smooth as velvet, inescapable as
a rip tide. It had been like this nearly seven years ago—
fire and ice, a turbulent, all-consuming need that still echoed through every cell in her body.

Did she dare? Patric had made no guarantees—and of
course he couldn't.

But perhaps—and for the first time she allowed herself
to articulate the thought—perhaps this could be a true new
beginning.

It was a gamble that would play with hearts—her own
and Nick's—but it would be cowardly to give up the
chance to love Patric, to build some sort of future with
him.

A sparrow chose that moment to land on the edge of
the table—a sophisticated, worldly sparrow, with a good
eye for food and danger. Nick froze; from the corner of
her eye Kate saw the small bird hop twice and pick up a
crumb.

Caught in a web of thick silence, walled off by Patric's
intense, devouring gaze from the laughter and noise of the
people all around them, she jumped when a seagull cried—
raucous, infinitely forlorn. Startled, the sparrow flew away,

and reality crashed into that hushed, enchanted, sensual world.

Stunned by its power, Kate dragged her gaze away.

When Nick enthused, 'Did you see that, Mum? Did you see that, Mr Sutherland?' she could only nod and wait for her spinning heart to settle down.

After Kate had finished her coffee they set off for the playground. At first Nick couldn't resist showing off, but soon his interest in the climbing bars took over and he began to concentrate on what he was doing.

'You don't seem alarmed by his daring,' Patric remarked as Nick swung across the bars.

They were seated at a picnic table close by. Kate said, 'Fussing drives him crazy. He doesn't like pain, so he's reasonably sensible—or as sensible as a child of his age can be. Because I don't often make a fuss he's inclined to listen when I do. And I watch him like a hawk.'

'You must have found it hard at first.'

She didn't lie. 'Yes,' she said. 'Having to surrender my entire life to another person, even my own child, was a real struggle.'

His expression didn't alter. 'From high school to motherhood in one huge leap. A quick lesson in maturity,' he said.

'Oh, indeed,' she said drily. It was probably just as well that she found it difficult to remember that year.

Patric's hand tightened into a fist against the rough boards of the table. Almost immediately the long fingers straightened, but that momentary lapse of control left her obscurely comforted.

She said, 'Nick was worth it.'

'Children having children is not usually good for the parent or the child,' he said austerely. 'You've done well with Nick, but at what cost to yourself? Working in a dress shop is not the career in management you wanted.'

'Without qualifications there isn't much choice,' she said bluntly. 'Anyway, I don't plan to stay in the shop for the rest of my life. Next year I'm going to start extramural studies.' It was a decision she hadn't even realised she'd made.

'Good. What made you come to Whangarei?'

Kate fixed her eyes on her son. 'I didn't want to stay in Christchurch, and any flat I could afford in Auckland was in an area I didn't want my child to grow up in.' Besides, in Auckland there had always been the remote possibility that she might run into Sean. Or Patric. 'So I looked around for a small city. Whangarei was going through a hard time then, and there was plenty of cheap accommodation.'

'You must have been lonely.'

'I soon made friends.'

'You always had friends,' he said. 'Yet I used to think that, although you were genuinely fond of them, you kept some part of yourself detached.'

Startled, she asked, 'Was I so cold and withdrawn?'

'Far from it—it was obvious that you liked your friends.' He paused, then resumed deliberately, 'You were essentially self-contained. You still are.'

Happily swinging from the bars, Nick waved; she waved back. 'I don't know where you got that idea. No one is self-contained.'

'I watched you grow up,' he said, his voice reflective. 'You were an enchanting girl, but I thought there was something wrong with me for being so fascinated by a girl so young. Especially when she obviously wasn't in the least interested in me.'

This surprised a sardonic laugh from Kate. 'Of course I was—every girl in Poto over the age of twelve was in love with you. You must have known.'

Drily cynical, he said, 'In love with love. Or more likely in love with the Sutherland name and the Sutherland assets.'

Kate turned her head. He'd been watching Nick too, but now he parried her gaze with cool, guarded eyes. Such iron discipline must have been learned in a hard school, she thought, astounded by her anger. It was ridiculous to feel protective of Patric Sutherland.

'You don't believe that,' she scoffed.

'I've had it pointed out to me by experts,' he said, sarcasm curling through his tone, flicking against each word.

'Who?'

'My father, mainly.'

Shocked, she said, 'Why on earth—?'

'On my eighteenth birthday he took me aside and explained that as I was going to take over Sutherland Aviation I was what he called "a good catch". I told you he was old-fashioned.' He spoke levelly, without inflection. 'According to him, women would do their best to lure me into relationships, not because they were attracted to me personally but because they wanted access to my bank balance.'

Kate thought of Patric's father, a tall man with a handsome face and a quick wit. Fiercely wishing she could have just five minutes with Alex Sutherland, she said, 'How ridiculous! You had a lot more going for you than your parents' money—'

He turned his head and smiled—not a pleasant smile. 'Sweet Kate,' he said evenly. 'He was right. Although she'd have denied it, that's what Laura wanted.'

She protested, 'You can't have thought the only reason you were so popular was money!'

'It helped,' he said calmly, stating a fact. 'It always helps.'

In Kate's mind he'd been the golden man—beloved of the gods, her chosen one.

It had been hero-worship. During their exquisitely drawn-out courtship they'd talked of many things—of their hopes and aspirations, of their fears and the things they loved and hated—but now she realised that she'd known very little about the man who'd taken her virginity. Known little and understood less.

She glanced at his profile, implacable against the fresh green of the park, and as if she'd spoken he turned. Desire bridged the space between them, raw and primitive, as inexorable and dangerously seductive as lava hot from the heart of the earth.

Dry-mouthed, Kate could only stare.

He asked harshly, 'What is it, do you think? Why, after all these years, and other women, do you still have the power to drive me to the edge of insanity? When you came towards me in that theme park on the Gold Coast I literally couldn't breathe; I had to force myself to move, to go to you, and it took all of my self-control not to kiss you with years of need and hunger.'

'Other women?' she asked quickly, jealously.

His smile was cold, almost aggressive. 'Oh, yes. After Laura died I looked for you again, but you'd dropped off the face of the earth.'

He looked back at Nick, still swinging on bars, scarlet-faced now. He'd stop soon, Kate thought.

'Do you know how many Browns there are in New Zealand?' Patric asked, an emotion close to contempt chilling his voice. 'Tens of thousands. I finally accepted that you'd meant what you'd said that day in Tatamoa. It seemed ludicrous to remain faithful to someone who'd turned me down so comprehensively, so I didn't. However, I have little taste for promiscuity and I'm not careless. Have you had any other lovers?'

It was none of his business. 'No.'

His austere face hardened. 'Why?'

Nothing but the truth would do. 'Because I couldn't bear to be touched.'

His expression froze. He scrutinised her face as though he'd never seen her before. Kate braced herself, but he didn't speak. Instead he reached across the rough, weather-stained wood of the table and took her hand in his. The exquisite pleasure of it almost shattered her.

Until then she'd been able to delude herself that she had

some control over the situation, but once Patric touched her she went up in flames for him like tinder in the desert, like an unstable explosive needing only a spark to set it off.

'Can you bear that?' he asked, demanding her surrender.

She wasn't prepared to give it to him. Locked in his long fingers, hers quivered.

'Kate?'

Reluctantly she said, 'I'm not screaming.'

'Your pulse is fluttering.' With his other hand he pressed the tips of her fingers against the veins in his wrist. Beneath them his pulse thundered. In a voice that compelled belief, he said, 'It's like that for me too, Kate, so it's just as well we met again. If we hadn't, we'd both have spent a lifetime searching for each other, only to go desperate and alone into our graves.'

It was too soon, she thought confusedly, looking into a face that might have been hewn in granite.

'Mummy?'

Nick's interruption, a difficult blend of concern and demand, broke the spell. With the wildfire colour of sexual awareness still burning her cheeks, she turned to greet her son; without haste Patric let go her hand and got to his feet.

Nick looked from one to the other. 'Why were you holding his hand?' he asked, his tone balanced on the edge of belligerence. 'Is he going to be my uncle, like Jason's uncle?'

'No,' Patric said coolly, 'I am not.'

'Then why were you holding his hand? You don't hold anyone else's hand.'

Kate stood up too. 'I was holding Mr Sutherland's hand because I like to, and I think we'd better be getting back home,' she said cravenly.

Both Patric and Nick glanced at her. Clearly masculine attitudes outranked genetics, because for a second they looked oddly alike, brows drawn into a knot, both gazes straight and intent.

Then they moved, and that fleeting likeness vanished. Nick came forward and took her hand. Kate thought Patric was going to walk on the other side of her; she was relieved when he took up his position so that they had Nick in the middle.

With an understanding of male psychology she applauded, Patric distracted Nick by asking, 'Who's the wing in your team—the redheaded boy?'

'Timmy Blunt.' Nick relaxed visibly. 'He's cool.'

'I liked the way he passed to you instead of keeping the ball to himself. He plays like a grown-up.'

As she listened to them discuss the prowess of several members of the team, Kate blessed the power of rugby on New Zealand males. When Patric let drop that he had not only met the All Blacks—New Zealand's highly successful national rugby team—but was a personal friend of the captain, Nick's resentment vanished and he plied this heroic being with questions.

Unbidden, into Kate's mind once again sneaked the thought that Patric would make a wonderful father. Nick said something and Patric laughed with him, and for a moment she was torn by anguish.

Oh, he'd probably be tough, but his children would know exactly where they stood with him—and he'd be fair—and they'd never grow up doubting his love for them.

CHAPTER EIGHT

It was three o'clock when they reached home; after a stealthy glance at her watch Kate asked Patric whether he'd like to come in for coffee.

'No, thank you,' he replied. 'I have a meeting in Wellington on Monday morning, and I need to get some work done for it.'

Stifling a raw disappointment, she said sedately, 'Then thank you very much for lunch and a lovely day.'

From the back came Nick's voice. 'Yes, thank you, Mr Sutherland.'

Patric didn't answer immediately; Kate's muscles tightened, but when he turned his head to smile at the boy in the back seat she relaxed. She must have imagined that second of taut silence.

'I forgot to thank you for your answer to my postcard,' he said. 'It was a great letter, and I really enjoyed reading it. I'd like to come up next Saturday. Where do you play, Nick, and what time?'

'Kamo,' Nick said, adding a little uncertainly, 'Nine o'clock, isn't it, Mummy?'

'Yes.'

'I'll pick you up,' Patric said, and then, 'What's the matter?' as Kate shook her head.

'I'm taking a carload of children,' she said.

'So what's the problem?' His voice was tinged with impatience. 'This car can pick up kids as well as your Mini. Better, in fact, because we can fit more in. What time do you usually set off?'

Kate's hackles rose; he was taking too much for granted. Without giving herself time to think, she said evenly, 'You don't need to, Patric. We'll see you at Kamo.' Keeping her voice steady and unemotional, she gave him directions to the sports ground and opened her door. 'Come on, Nick.'

Patric's brows lifted, but he made no attempt to persuade her; clearly he didn't view this as a battle worth fighting. 'If you can organise someone to stay with Nick we could go out to dinner on Saturday night.'

He had tact, because Nick would have objected to the word babysitter. As it was her son's face stiffened, and he gave her the glare that indicated hurt feelings. 'I don't want you to go out,' he said bluntly.

Kate would have liked a chance to think the invitation over, but Nick's possessive response made up her mind instantly. Ignoring him, she said, 'I'd like that. What time?'

'Shall we say six-thirty? Would that suit you?'

'Seven-thirty would be better—I have to feed Nick.' Even so, it would be much earlier, she suspected with a hidden gleam of amusement, than Patric normally ate.

He walked them up the front path, waited while Kate opened the door, smiled at her and the still simmering Nick, then said, 'I'll see you next Saturday,' and left them.

He looked like a god, Kate thought foolishly, tall and confident, striding down the narrow path with an inherent, masculine grace that spoke of strength and control and dynamic power. The car door closed softly behind him.

After a moment of indecision, Nick waved. A lean hand lifted from the wheel in a cool, impersonal response as the car drew away, leaving Kate astonished and wary and excited.

She wasn't granted the luxury of examining her feelings because Nick immediately demanded, 'Why can't *I* go to dinner with you? I had to stay behind in Australia too!'

'We'll be back late—well after your bedtime.' Kate's voice was firm. Sweet-tempered though he was, when her son set his mind on something he applied constant pressure. The only way to deal with him was a pleasant, unmoved refusal to give in.

'I'll be good,' he promised now, obviously settling in for the long haul.

Kate said cheerfully, 'I don't recollect Mr Sutherland asking you.'

This threw Nick for a second, until he thought of a clincher. 'He would've if you'd said I could come.'

'He wouldn't have, because he knows that boys your age should be in bed early. Otherwise,' she added cunningly, 'they don't grow properly. How do you think Mr Sutherland got to be as tall and big as he is? Not by staying up late when he was almost six years old, I can tell you.'

And, disregarding the hot little tremor that slithered down her spine at the thought of Patric's height and those wide shoulders, she closed the door behind them and put her bag down.

Temporarily diverted, Nick said, 'I bet he could be an All Black if he wanted to. Why do you think he isn't one, Mummy?'

Kate laughed; to small New Zealand boys an All Black was next to the angels. 'I don't know. Perhaps he wasn't good enough.'

But Nick was having none of this. 'He would be,' he said indignantly. 'P'raps he hurt his leg or something. Mummy, can I go over to Rangi's place and play with his computer?'

'We're going there for dinner tonight,' Kate reminded him. 'You'll be able to play with it then. Why don't you cut me a lettuce from the garden? The big Iceberg would be best. I'm going to make a salad to take with us. Make sure you hold the knife the way I showed you.'

Being trusted to use a knife was a big deal, and Nick took his responsibilities very seriously. Kate watched from the window as he carefully cut through the stem of the lettuce, jaw angled, black hair gleaming in the fickle spring sun. When it was done he stood up and grinned at her, filled with triumph. An inconvenient blast of maternal love shook her. Did she have the right to set off down a path that might hurt them both?

Her volatile emotions seesawed between fierce protectiveness and her long-suppressed hunger for the fulfilment—sexual, emotional and mental—that only Patric had ever been able to give her.

As Nick came towards the back door, Kate wondered whether she was trying unconsciously to revert to the girl she'd been before Sean Cusack's brutality had shattered some fundamental trust in her. Was her response to Patric a hold-over from the past, rooted in her longing to wipe out the attack?

Ah, no. She had only to recall the way Patric's touch had affected her—talk about sensual overload! The physical hunger was real and honest. For the rest—only time would tell.

'Great,' she said as Nick came carefully through the door. 'Would you like to make the dressing?'

While he measured the ingredients for the dressing she ran the lettuce under the tap.

How badly hurt would Nick be if the affair died into nothingness? Perhaps she should take no risks at all, flag away any chance of fulfilment until he'd left home.

Twelve years from now; she'd be thirty-six.

It would be simpler if she could fool herself into thinking that Patric might have marriage in mind.

Perhaps he did. Could she marry him? A feverish, compelling hunger arced through her. Only, she thought stoutly, if she was sure he loved Nick.

'It's ready,' Nick said, breaking into her depressing thoughts. He set down the jar and grinned. 'Do I have to go and wash?'

'You look pretty clean to me. How about tidying up your bedroom?' She folded an old, thin teatowel around the lettuce and set off to swing it outside.

He groaned, but asked, 'Mummy?'

She recognised that tone. 'Mmm?'

'Do you think Mr Sutherland knew these are my new shirt and trousers?'

'He might not have realised they were new,' Kate said practically, 'but I'm sure he noticed how good you looked.'

He nodded and went into his room.

The lettuce-filled cloth swished through the air, spraying drops of water across the small lawn as Kate admired the fat crimson buds on Anna's climbing rose.

Patric had chosen the right time to ask her to go out with him—taking her by surprise and demanding a quick answer. And even if Nick hadn't shown that worrying possessiveness she probably would have agreed, because she wanted to go out to dinner with him.

Oh, face facts; she wanted *much* more than that.

Damn the man, she thought crossly. Why had he seen her in that theme park and tipped her life upside down?

Nick called from the steps, 'I'm ready to go now.'

'Have you tidied your bedroom?'

'I picked up my toys,' he said virtuously.

Kate glanced at her watch. 'We've still got some time. Why don't you write a letter to thank Mr Sutherland for lunch, and I'll put it in with mine?'

'All right,' he said, disappearing back inside.

Kate crouched to smell the last exquisitely scented freesias; at the evocative, poignant perfume the past surged over her in a titanic wave of mingled joy and grief and despair.

Somehow she and Patric were linked; if she wanted freedom from that emotional tie she was going to have to follow this through. He'd been right when he'd told her she was imprisoned in the past. In many ways she'd progressed no further than the naïve eighteen-year-old who'd been seduced with ravishingly tender passion by her fairytale prince and then brutalised by the villain.

The experience had left her locked into a frustrated, obsessive desire. Get that out of the way and perhaps—just perhaps—she might be able to meet Patric on equal terms.

Saturday found both she and Nick prickly with anticipation. Bubbling with excitement, he sat beside her in the front of the Mini as it filled up with two other children.

When they reached the sports ground Kate's heart ached at his swift glance around the small group of parents and children. Nick gave no indication that he was disappointed not to see Patric—that wasn't his way—but his mother knew.

Five minutes after the game started she heard her name. Colour heated her skin as she turned and saw Patric. He was smiling, and his eyes gleamed with a dangerous metallic sheen.

Kate's heart leapt into her throat. 'Hello,' she said, adding inanely, 'You got here.'

'I had excellent instructions,' he said, his smile widening a fraction as he stopped beside her. 'You look like spring.'

The sunlit air danced before her eyes, lighting a slow, untamed fire within her. Forcing herself to remember that there were people—friends, interested onlookers—standing close by, she said demurely, 'Thank you. Did you have a good trip up?'

'I was surprised at the traffic, which is why I'm late. Auckland must have decided to go north for the day.'

For a second—for a fraction of a second—she tensed, overwhelmed by his size, his dominating physical impact, the way he shut out everyone else. It would be too easy to let herself lean on that masculine strength, but for all their sakes she had to keep her independence.

'Thank you for the letter,' he said. 'Nick writes very well for a six-year-old.'

Pride glowed within her. 'He does, doesn't he? His teacher says he's extremely bright.' She laughed a little.

'But never tell him that—he thinks he's pretty near perfect.'

'Most children of his age find it difficult to accept that they have faults, I suspect.' Patric's voice was amused as they both turned to the game. The tension of their last meeting dissipated in eager encouragement as the two teams of small boys tussled for supremacy on the muddy field.

The game over, and the required cheers given and received, Kate watched as Nick, crimson-cheeked and mud-streaked, rushed across. 'Hello, Mr Sutherland,' he shouted as he reached them.

'Hello, Nick. You played well.'

It was clearly an accolade of the highest order, and Nick flushed even more hotly. 'I didn't get a try.'

'No, but you stayed in position and passed the ball so that the man outside you scored. That was good team play.'

Nick nodded. 'I remembered what you told me. Sister Mary-Louise said I played well.'

'Is she your coach?'

'Yes. She's cool.' Nick jumped in the air for sheer excitement. 'She can kick the ball further than the big boys.'

While Kate collected her passengers Nick and Patric walked ahead, Nick fizzing with delight, Patric smiling and relaxed. As they came up to the car, one of the boys with her asked Kate, 'Is that Nick's father?'

These children knew the realities of modern relationships. 'No, he's a friend,' Kate said.

Patric gave her a level, enigmatic glance that shivered through to her toes. Parrying it with an impersonal smile, she unlocked the doors, saying, 'OK, in you get, and make sure you do those seatbelts up.'

'I'll see you back at the house,' Patric said.

Kate nodded and got into the car. Twenty minutes later, both boys delivered into their parents' custody, she headed for home.

'One more game to go,' Nick observed, squirming beneath the seatbelt. 'If it's warm enough we can go swimming at the beginning of next month. Do you think my old togs will fit me?'

'Probably not, so you'll be able to wear your new ones.'

Next month was November, and then—too soon—it would be Christmas. Sometimes she and Nick went up to Kerikeri to spend it with her cousin, but this year Juliet and her family were going to the South Island to spend the holiday with her sister Jenny. Anticipation, keen as a needle, stirred in the pit of Kate's stomach. What would Patric be doing this Christmas?

'I'll ask Mr Sutherland if I can come with you tonight,' Nick said casually as they swung into their small street. 'Rangi won't mind if I don't stay with him. You can ring him up and tell him.'

'It would be incredibly rude of you to break your word to Rangi,' Kate said calmly. 'And even ruder to go where you haven't been invited.'

He sent her a darkling look, and would have returned to the fray if Patric hadn't been waiting for them outside the house.

He got out of the car as they came up, and smiled down at Nick. 'Where would you like to go to lunch?' he asked, and Nick forgot about his campaign for the present.

They went to a fast-food restaurant. Sitting opposite Patric, Kate realised with a small shock that he didn't seem out of place amongst the noisy families and silent elderly couples; he had a rare ability to dominate his surroundings, mould them to fit him.

After Nick had eaten his fill they visited the Clock Museum. Apparently as intrigued as Nick with the splendid array of clocks, Patric answered her determined, curious, fascinated son's questions, patiently explaining how the clocks worked, entering into his enthusiasm—and listening when Nick told him all he'd learned about wave action.

Perhaps his attitude was a carry-over from his initial belief that Nick was his son. Or perhaps he really liked children. Kate tried very hard not to build too much on it.

When at last they came out into the sunlight Nick asked, 'Can we go to the Museum of Fishes?'

Kate glanced at her watch and shook her head. 'We have to go now.'

Nick opened his mouth to protest, then thought better of it. 'All right,' he said, adding with his best smile, 'We can go there next time, can't we?'

'We'll see,' Kate said noncommittally. She turned to Patric. 'Where are we eating tonight? I'll need to leave the phone number with Ngaire MacArthur.'

'It's a place called Seabird.'

'I haven't heard of that one,' she said. 'It must be new.'

'It's not in Whangarei,' he said calmly, 'It's in the Bay of Islands.'

An hour's drive to the north. Flustered, Kate said, 'Oh. All right.'

At five o'clock she delivered Nick, with his favourite green dinosaur and a bag of necessities, to the MacArthurs' house.

'He seems a bit down,' Ngaire said, watching him with a critical eye. 'Everything all right?'

'He wants to come too,' Kate said with a wry smile. She handed over a sheet of paper with the name of the restaurant and the number.

Ngaire's eyes widened. 'So do I,' she said with feeling. 'That place is supposed to be absolutely gorgeous—very exclusive—and the food spectacularly wonderful. Who are you going out with?'

'An old friend.'

When Ngaire looked thoughtfully at Nick, disappearing rapidly through a door with the two youngest MacArthurs, Kate added hastily, 'No.'

'Pity,' Ngaire said cheerfully. 'Oh, well, have a great

time. Nick and Rangi will. Just don't get here tomorrow morning before nine, OK?'

Kate laughed. 'I promise.'

She'd never been allowed to forget that the first time Nick had stayed with the happy, noisy, chaotic MacArthurs she'd arrived at eight next morning to pick him up. He and two of the boys had been ensconced in front of the television, eating an eclectic breakfast as they watched a video, while everyone else enjoyed their Sunday lie-in.

Ngaire gave her a swift, perceptive glance. 'Have fun,' she said. 'You deserve it. One day Nick's going to grow up and leave you, and if you haven't made yourself a life by then you'll miss him unbearably.'

Her friend's injunction hit uncomfortably close to home. 'I know.'

'Besides,' Ngaire said with ruthless practicality, 'It's not good for boys to grow up believing they're the one shining star in their mother's heaven, even if they are. It makes them arrogant and dissatisfied, because no woman is going to live up to the adoring mother who loves them unconditionally.'

But Patric—the focus of his parents' hopes and love and aspirations, their golden son—hadn't grown up arrogant and dissatisfied. Of course their love hadn't been unconditional; they'd more or less forced him to marry Laura.

Kate wondered how much persuasion had been needed; Laura had been an extraordinarily beautiful woman— lushly sophisticated even as an adolescent.

'And wives no longer love unconditionally,' Ngaire went on. 'If they get treated badly they take off—and so they should. I don't think you need to worry about Nick, though. In spite of that determined chin, he's a love. He'll be all right. Now off you go and get yourself pretty for tonight.'

Nick reappeared on a wave of children and dogs to give her a swift hug. Without a trace of regret he said, 'Yes, you have a good time, Mummy. Bye.'

Kate spent the next half-hour dithering in front of her wardrobe. The top and trousers she'd selected looked good on her, but somehow didn't seem entirely suitable for a place as chic and exclusive as Seabird.

In the end she wore them because they were the most sophisticated clothes she possessed. The soft mesh-knit top in her favourite pale green, with no sleeves and a deep vee neck, revealed a lot of skin. Dreamed up by a designer famous for his slinky, erotic clothes, it was meant to be worn without lining or bra, which was probably why it hadn't sold. After Kate had bought it in the shop's sale she'd searched until she found silk the exact shade of her skin and had carefully sewn a lining into it.

Kate pulled it over her head and settled it around her shoulders, eyeing the slight swell of her breasts beneath the material. 'It's perfectly decent,' she told her reflection in the small mirror.

Complementing the top were silk trousers—loosely fitting and with a faintly oriental air. Another reason for the ensemble not to sell—it was difficult to classify; too informal in design for the occasions its cut and superb material suggested, and youthful yet expensive. Kate had loved it on sight.

How glad she was that the boutique owner had allowed her delight with the outfit to override her commercial instincts! Otherwise Kate would have had to go out with Patric in clothes chosen for their practicality and hard-wearing qualities.

What would he think when he saw her?

Ruthlessly subduing the hot excitement that clutched her stomach, she checked herself in the mirror. She'd left her face naked except for a slick of lipgloss, slightly darker than her skin, and a hint of gentle shadow to emphasise her eyes. The tunic probably should have earrings to set it off, or a thin gold chain around her neck, but she had neither.

She tied the thick, slippery mass of her hair back with

a satin ribbon the same subtle green as her clothes. Picking up the narrow clutch that doubled as her evening bag, she slid her feet into low-heeled black pumps and set her chin.

As the doorbell pealed colour drained from her face. You fool, common sense said calmly. You should never have agreed to this.

Perhaps common sense was right, but a flame of rebellion in her ignored that dreary, sensible announcement. She'd been sensible for almost seven long years; it was past time to accept the challenges life offered.

CHAPTER NINE

ALTHOUGH informal, Patric's clothes were tailored for his lean body, their skilful cut and fine materials emphasising wide, masculine shoulders, narrow hips and long, heavily muscled legs. After a quick, intent survey of her face he said quietly, 'You look like Melusina—a very young Melusina.'

A shift of perception—subtle but irreversible—took place within Kate. Suddenly free, almost as though he had somehow managed to strike invisible, unfelt shackles from her soul, she felt light, buoyant—floating in a sea of expectation, of hope.

'Who was Melusina?' she asked, locking the door behind her.

He took her arm and walked her towards the gate, keeping position so that she stayed on the narrow concrete path while he was on the grass. 'A French water spirit. Of course she was exquisitely beautiful. She fell in love with a French noble and married him on condition that he should never see her on a Saturday.'

'So he promised faithfully never to peep on a Saturday, but he couldn't resist the temptation?'

'Naturally,' he said drily. 'And like all people who pry he suffered for it, because she wasn't human, she was a serpent. Or a mermaid—history's not exactly clear. Whatever, she fled from him, and he spent the rest of his life mourning her.'

'A mermaid has charisma,' Kate said thoughtfully, 'but I don't think I like being compared to a serpent. And you'd think these mythical characters—Melusina and Bluebeard and their ilk—would learn from each other. Nothing whets a human's curiosity more than being told not to do something—it's practically an open invitation.'

He laughed and put her into the car. Once they were heading northward through Whangarei's quiet suburbs, he said, 'They were a stupid lot. And if she was a serpent, I'm sure Melusina was an infinitely seductive and alluring serpent with no idea of her power. A siren, like you.' Beneath the deep, smoothly sensual voice prowled latent emotion, edgy with the leashed violence of desire.

An answering wildness flared into life inside her, straining against the bars that will-power and discipline imposed on her emotions and her thoughts.

Unsteadily she said, 'Thank you, I think.'

Patric smiled but his voice was satirical. 'As the Americans say, you're welcome.'

Lights swung towards the car, swished by, and dwindled into a blur of brilliant red as the vehicle purred through the night. Tension stretched between them, a stark, dancing force that pulsated with unspoken thoughts, unbidden feelings, runaway sensations.

He broke into the silence. 'Your eyes are so clear, yet they hide secrets. Seven years ago I wanted to find out what those secrets were. I still do.'

A momentary flash of fear kicked in the pit of her stomach. Swiftly, almost airily, she got out, 'Everyone has things they'd rather not talk about.'

'Of course,' he said, his voice even, almost expressionless, 'but in those days I was desperate to know what you thought and felt. I suppose I hoped understanding you would give me some power.'

'Power?' She was shocked.

'Oh, yes.' He gave her a sardonic, almost angry glance. 'Didn't you realise, Kate? I was utterly defenceless and I hated it—it had never happened to me before. I couldn't get enough of you, yet I knew you were too young to make any sort of commitment. Most of all I wanted to know whether you felt the same way about me.'

'You must have known I did,' she protested, thinking back to the transparent child she'd been.

'How could I? I knew you liked me, but you seemed to like everyone. You were always unfailingly kind—to the local kids, to anyone who stayed at Tatamoa. You gave them the gift of your smile and your interest, and left them all wanting more. Girls liked you too, although they were baffled by your refusal to join in their ploys and games. You were even kind to my contemptible cousin Sean before he tried to kiss you.'

Kate stared blindly into the dark. This was what it must be like to walk on the lip of a volcano, knowing that one slip could lead to disaster. Swallowing the coppery taste in her mouth, she said the only thing she could think of. 'That last year I was just an ordinary girl well out of her depth.'

'Hardly. Ordinary girls flirted and fluttered their eyelashes and posed elegantly in their briefest clothes. You went serenely on your way. All that summer I wondered whether it was my imagination—and hormones—that made me believe you felt more for me than for anyone else. Until we made love. I knew then—or thought I knew.'

Kate's skin tightened. What had he learned then—that she was totally, completely in love with him? That she had no defence against his experienced sexuality?

'The world stopped for me,' he said roughly. 'You blew my mind away with your sweet passion. I shouldn't have made love to you, but I didn't have the self-control to pull back. Did I frighten you so much that you couldn't bear to see me again, Kate?'

'No,' she said in a low voice. 'Of course you didn't.'

His mouth thinned. 'I couldn't think of any other reason for you to break it off.'

'I was very depressed that term at Christchurch,' she said, choosing her words carefully. Numbed by shock and an all-pervading sense of degradation, for three months she'd been lost in pain.

In her innermost heart, beneath the dreams and the desire and the heat of love, Kate had known—had understood since before their first kiss—that she wasn't fit for life as Patric's wife. Kind though his parents had been to their farm manager's niece, they certainly didn't want their son to marry her. Intelligence and common sense weren't all that were necessary in the world over which Pilar Sutherland held sway. Sophistication and the gloss of social confidence, of knowing what to do and how to do it, were every bit as important.

Sean's threats had sickened her and humiliated her. 'I'll tell Patric,' he'd taunted, his handsome, fleshy face filled with a despicable glee. 'I might let him marry you—and wouldn't that give Laura a kick in the teeth, stuck-up bitch!—but sooner or later I'll tell him that I've had you. He's a possessive bastard and he hates me, so that's going to really get him where it hurts!'

He would have done it, and she couldn't have allowed herself to be the weakness that exposed Patric to that humiliation.

Disgusted and shamed, she couldn't have gone to him carrying Sean's child in her womb.

After that last, shattering meeting with Patric she'd gone back to Christchurch because it was as far away as she could get from Tatamoa. Then, mercifully, the physical and hormonal changes of pregnancy had taken her over, driving everything but the need for survival from her mind; in the end it had simply been easier to turn her back on the whole situation and strike out unencumbered by the weight of the past.

In a toneless voice Patric said, 'I've always felt I abandoned you when I left Tatamoa the day after we'd made love.'

Had she blamed him for abandoning her? Oh, not for going to his father, no, never that! But after Patric left his cousin had come to Tatamoa, lured her to the homestead with the promise of a letter from Patric, and raped her.

Had she somehow blamed him for not protecting her?

No. Sean was responsible for his own actions.

Coughing to overcome the ache in her throat, she said, 'Your father was dying! Of course I didn't expect you to dance attendance on me. You had to go. By May I knew— I was—' Her voice splintered. She dragged in a deep, impeded breath. 'Patric, I couldn't marry you when I was pregnant with another man's child.'

Hands gripping the wheel, he steered the car around one of Northland's notorious curves. Silence enveloped them, a silence thick with old pain. Kate realised she was holding her breath. A car sprang out of the darkness; in the glare of its lights Patric's face was revealed—icily rigid, each muscle clenched as though he was in intolerable anguish. Kate flinched, then shielded her eyes as the oncoming lights flicked onto full and down again.

'Patric—'

But he'd already dipped their lights. The oncoming car gave a swift toot on the horn as it surged past them.

Kate exhaled. She should let him concentrate on his driving; it was so unlike him to forget to dip.

He said harshly, 'I would have married you, Kate. I wanted to marry you more than anything in the world. I only married Laura—' He stopped and swore, his voice hoarse with anger. 'Why didn't you tell me?' he demanded between his teeth. 'Kate, you must have known I wouldn't blame you.'

No, but how would he have dealt with the knowledge that his cousin had raped her? What would it have done to a family already agonised by the prospect of Alex Sutherland's death? Because if they'd married sooner or later Sean's malice would have spilled over and he'd have told Patric, smashing any prospect of a future for them.

Noiseless, desperate words rasped her throat. Swallowing them, forbidding them life, she said, 'I was

damaged, Patric—too hurt and degraded to know what I
was doing. Anyway, even without...even if nothing had
happened it wouldn't have worked, you and I. I was far
too young; I didn't know how to be any sort of wife, especially not for a man in your position.'

'You'd have coped.' Although his voice was level, the
words were rasped by a raw undertone. 'I'd trust you to
deal with anything! Look at the way you managed with
Nick.'

'I had only one demanding male to deal with,' she returned, trying to lighten the atmosphere. 'The past's past.
Let's leave it there.'

A scurry of rain spattered against the windscreen. For
several minutes they drove without speaking, until he said
with a compelling intensity, 'Kate, I want very much to
leave the past where it belongs, as long as my future has
you in it.'

Kate's heart stopped in her chest. She stole a sideways
glance. His profile, starkly outlined against the night outside, was a silhouette of strength—straight forehead, the
sweep of nose, the male beauty of his mouth and the uncompromising determination of jaw and chin. Kate had
expected him to suggest an affair. Unless she was mis-
taken, he was offering her much more.

She stared down at her hands, knuckles gleaming white
in a frozen clasp. 'I—would like that too.'

Her voice sounded oddly muted, almost shaky. Scared.

Without taking his eyes off the road, Patric found her
hand and lifted it to his mouth, pressing a kiss to the palm
before replacing it in her lap. 'This time I won't make the
mistake of valuing money and power over you,' he said
uncompromisingly.

'You didn't,' she said, trying to repress the shiver of
delight that ran through her. 'You put one sort of love over
another, and I understand. It would have been cruel to defy
your father when he was so ill. I imagine he knew that

Sutherland Aviation needed both you and Laura's father—
he must have been desperately worried.'

'That was no excuse for blackmailing me,' he said, his
voice grim. 'And even less excuse for me to give in to it.
I've learned my lesson, Kate. Now, tell me what you've
been doing these last few years.'

Relieved, she gave him a quick rundown on her life—
skipping the worst bits, making him smile by recounting
several of Nick's more memorable exploits—and as the
minutes slipped by and the traffic thinned out tension began to seep from her. By the time they reached the star-
silvered Bay of Islands she was filled with a bright, fragile
hope.

That night Patric wooed her with his attention, with his
voice, with his eyes—narrowed and intent—and with his
conversation.

Over the ambrosial food, in surroundings of quiet, restrained sophistication looking out onto shimmering, is-
land-dotted waters, she finally surrendered completely to
that helpless, helter-skelter, headlong tumble into love,
with its terrors and its singing, piercing hunger—both
physical and emotional—and the fierce elation that came
from exploring Patric's keen, disciplined mind and personality.

And always, always beneath the stimulating conversation and the potent communication of eyes raced a current
of need, glittering and powerful and intense, marooning
her on the cusp between frustration and fulfilment.

Later, outside her unit, he walked her to the door while
a slow excitement built within her. He knew Nick wasn't
there...

'You've made a pretty garden,' he said.

Its scents floated around them; the wet fragrance of new-
mown grass, a fugitive sweetness of flowers, some intense,
spicy perfume she'd never smelt before.

'With Anna and Ngaire's help.' Her voice sounded flat,

almost strained. Without looking at him she unlocked the door.

Patric came in with her and checked out each room.

'It's perfectly safe,' Kate said on a half-laugh when they stood together in the cramped sitting room.

'I lost you once,' he said. 'I couldn't keep you safe then—I don't want the same thing to happen again.'

Without thinking she put her hand on his sleeve. 'It's over,' she said quietly, and for the first time she believed that it really was: the past had been faced, robbed of its capacity to hurt.

'Kate,' he said, and put his hands on her shoulders and bent to kiss her with a curbed passion.

Closing her eyes, Kate breathed in the scent and taste of him, the pressure of his hands, of his mouth, the reality of Patric Sutherland.

Desire coursed through her, hot and untamed and slow, and she could have cried out in rebellion when he lifted his head. Unevenly he said, 'I have to go back to Auckland tonight. I'll see you next weekend.'

Disappointed and surprised, she wondered why he'd pulled back. But she told herself they needed the breathing space. Yes, the past had been dealt with; now they needed to find the path to their future.

Yet in the following weeks that hunger grew into torment, intensifying each hour she spent with him, binding Kate with fragile, unbreakable chains until she thought the wanting would drive her crazy. Yet Patric's tenderness and restraint satisfied some long-lost part of her. She honoured him for his control; he was giving her time to overcome her natural fear about making love. It was as though they were reliving his first courtship, when she'd been barely more than a child, and he had moved from big brother to lover. So, although she relearned the strength and power of need and passion, she was content to travel slowly down the path to delight.

His tenderness when he touched her—the subtle mastery

of his hands on her skin, the fleeting, frequent caresses that were far from sexual yet set her on fire—showed that he was gentling her like a nervous filly. When they finally did make love she would be so attuned to him, to the thousand sensual signals of his body, that she wouldn't be repelled by his passion.

As spring warmed into summer he came north most weekends, and he rang several times a week, the calls becoming more intimate as they grew to know each other.

He continued to be, Kate thought, six weeks after that first dinner in the Bay of Islands as she watched him from the shelter of a sun umbrella, wonderful with her son. It didn't seem to worry him that Nick was the child of the man who had raped her—carefully, cleverly, he'd forged a friendship.

They were walking—the tall, impressive man, the lithe, quicksilver boy—along the foamy line where the waves washed onto the soft apricot sand. Occasionally Patric would crouch down level with Nick, and they'd pore over whatever took their interest. Nick had become fascinated by the idea of plants growing in the sea, so it was usually seaweed, but he was also collecting shells. When Kate saw their two heads so close together her heart shivered.

Tonight she and Patric were going out to dinner as they had most Saturdays since he'd come up the first time. Surely, she thought yearningly, he knew now that she wanted him—that she was ready for their relationship to deepen? How did you tell a man that without losing your dignity?

'You look funny,' Nick said, surprising her.

While she'd been lost in a daydream they'd come up, and were looking at her with the same quizzical expression.

'That's her mermaid smile,' Patric informed him.

Nick gave a crow of laughter. 'She hasn't got a tail.'

'Some mermaids look just like human beings,' Patric

said, his half-closed eyes sweeping Kate's legs, long and winter-pale. 'They're the dangerous ones.'

Need kicked her with exquisite precision in the pit of her stomach, drawing her down into a relentless longing. 'Don't talk about me as though I'm not here,' she said.

But Patric had seen her swift, involuntary shiver. Lashes drooping, he said in a voice roughened by a hidden hunger, 'The water's warm enough to swim in.' He held out his hand.

'Lovely.' Kate let him pull her to her feet.

He dropped his hand as soon as she was upright, but his index finger lingered across her palm.

She'd worn her togs beneath her shirt and shorts, and normally she wouldn't have been at all concerned about pulling her clothes off. However, that tiny, fleeting caress made her acutely self-conscious. Turning slightly under the pretence of supervising Nick, she stripped off her shorts; her bathing suit was old, but the dark green hugged her and she knew she looked good in it.

Without looking at Patric, she challenged Nick, 'Beat you in.'

'No, you won't,' he said, sprinting down the beach.

Kate set off after him, judging her speed so that they plunged into the surf at the same time. He loved the water, and was completely confident in it.

'Look!' he shouted, and dived down to Kate's feet, tickled her ankle and emerged, bubbling and boisterous, beside her.

'I thought you were a fish!'

He laughed. 'I caught a mermaid,' he said.

'No, only a mother,' Kate said, looking up.

At the sight of Patric, bronze shoulders gleaming in the sun, the water up to his black briefs, her brain shut down. He looked like something out of the dawn of time, she thought dazedly, all male, smoothly muscled and sleek and incredibly compelling.

'Did you see me, Mr Sutherland?' Nick's voice jarred

the silence. 'I dived down and touched Mummy's toes. I can dive off the edge of the pool, and when I'm eight she's going to show me how to dive off the boards. Mummy's the best diver in the world, except for the Olympics.'

Patric ruffled his hair. 'I know,' he said, and looked at Kate.

Who was standing there, mesmerised and mute, pulses thudding, mouth dry with apprehension and thirst as though she'd wandered in a desert these last years and now at last could see the feathery tips of palms above the burning sands. It took all of her will-power to free herself from Patric's sensual spell.

'I'm a good diver,' she managed, dragging her eyes away to gaze down at her son, 'but not that good.' And because she was exposing her emotions embarrassingly, she added, 'Come on, let's swim.'

She stayed with Nick, but Patric was never far away. Every time she looked up she met his eyes, glittering with the grey-black sheen of a gun barrel. He wasn't crudely obvious, but he used the games Nick insisted on as an excuse to touch her, addicting her further to his gentle caresses.

In the midst of a fast game of water tag Kate got caught by a larger than normal wave and tumbled over. Immediately, lean hands fastened onto her shoulders and pulled her upright, and while she stared into a face set and hard and possessive Patric bent and kissed her fiercely.

'I've run completely out of patience—I need you so much,' he muttered. 'Marry me, Kate.'

And when, thunderstruck, she couldn't answer, he said harshly, 'Please!'

Dimly her dazzled senses registered skin branded by his hands, by his mouth, and the distant sound of Nick's voice, backed by the impatient bray of a car horn on the road behind the beach. She looked into hot, resolute eyes, and flame seared across her, through her. 'Yes,' she said.

'Mummy?' Nick demanded. His wet hand slid into hers,

gripped. He said truculently, 'Did you get a mouthful of water?'

'No, I didn't. I don't breathe in when I go underwater,' she said, and managed a smile.

He glowered at her through wet, spiky lashes. 'Why did he kiss you like that?'

It was Patric who answered. 'Do you want a father, Nick?'

Nick turned his head. He stared up into Patric's controlled face, and after a long, charged moment nodded.

'Mothers and fathers kiss each other a lot,' Patric said coolly. 'I'm going to be your father from now on.'

Nick stared at him, then swivelled his eyes to Kate's face. 'Oh, all right,' he said offhandedly, reassured for the moment. 'Mr MacArthur kisses Rangi's mum all the time.' He touched Kate's arm. 'Bet you can't catch me,' he shouted, and duck-dived beneath the next wave.

Patric followed him, leaving Kate to gaze foolishly after them, her skin suddenly puckered with gooseflesh.

Leaving them to their game, she swam rapidly away from the beach, trying to work through bewilderment at the unexpected proposal. After a few minutes she heard Patric call her name, and realised she couldn't keep heading out to sea.

By the time she got back to them Patric had persuaded Nick out of the water and into his clothes. 'He was shivering,' he said, rubbing his own towel across his shoulders.

'Thank you,' she said lightly, keeping her eyes firmly away from him.

Nick peered at her. 'Dad wanted to go out to you, but I told him you were the best swimmer in the world,' he said proudly.

Kate's heart clenched. She looked at Patric, saw his smile, and had to blink to hide her tears.

'We thought Dad was what a boy of Nick's age should call his father,' he said. 'That's what Rangi calls his.'

'I know,' she said in a shaken voice, poised on a knife-

edge of disintegration. When Patric took Nick up to the
car, she dragged her clothes on and rubbed her face vigorously with the towel before following them. In the car
she covered her eyes with sunglasses.

'Would you get me mine, please?' Patric asked. 'In the
glovebox.'

She found them and handed them over, acutely con-
scious of the warmth of his fingers as he took them. In the
back seat Nick bounced around, talking almost non-stop.
None of them said a word about Patric's astounding dec-
laration. By the time they arrived home Kate was being
tormented by a mixture of shock and slow, pulsing joy.

In the house, she ordered Nick to the bathroom. 'Off
you go—now, right this minute, before you shed any more
sand on the floor.' Carefully avoiding Patric's eyes, she
asked politely, 'Would you like to shower here?'

'No, I'll go,' he said. Ignoring Nick's hovering presence, he lifted Kate's chin. His eyes were intent, probing,
and ruthless. 'Don't be late,' he commanded. 'I'll pick you
up at seven.'

'I'll be ready.'

From the doorway Nick asked, 'Can't I come too?'

'No,' Kate said, glad that he gave her the excuse to pull
away from Patric's too-forceful gaze. 'You have an ap-
pointment with Rangi.'

He chuckled, but insisted, 'You'll come and get me
early in the morning?'

'Promise,' Kate said, at the same time as Patric's short,
'Yes.'

Nick disappeared into the hall and Patric said, 'I'd better
go.'

Feeling cheated, Kate nodded. He traced the tiny frown
between her eyes and said, 'It'll be all right, Kate.'

'I know,' she said. 'He'll need to be reassured over and
over again, but he's happy about it.'

'Is that the only reason you're marrying me? Because
Nick's happy? There'll be times when he's not, Kate.'

'I know that. We'll deal with it. And, no, that's not why I said I'd marry you.' Now she knew how a woman told a man she wanted him. Reaching up, she kissed the triangle of tanned skin at the collar of his shirt. 'No,' she repeated against his skin, tasting him, breathing out on his wet skin.

His hand lifted her chin; transfixed by the blazing sensuality in his face, she'd barely begun to respond to the swift, searing kiss when he stepped back and said, 'I'll see you later,' and while she stared after him, the sound of the taps turned on full brought her back to herself.

When she went in to check Nick's cleanliness he presented her with a scrubbed and glistening face and demanded, 'Is he really, really going to be my father?'

'Yes,' she said.

Nick gave her one of his grave, unchildlike looks. 'Good,' he said. 'He knows about boys.'

'So he should. He used to be one himself.'

Nick grinned. 'Will I grow as big as him?'

'I don't know. My father was tall, and so was my mother, so although I'm not tall myself I might have handed on a few of those genes to you.'

Nodding, Nick said, 'I'd like to be tall as Mr Sutherland.' He hesitated, then added as though trying it out for sound, 'Dad.'

'Just be the best Nick Brown you can be,' she said, adding quickly, 'Bend your head forward so I can wash the salt and sand out of your hair.'

That night, with Nick safely ensconced at the MacArthurs' place, she put on the same outfit she'd worn the night Patric had taken her to dinner in the Bay of Islands. Such a short time ago, she realised with a vague sense of surprise.

Just six elongated weeks, each followed by a weekend that had gone by so fast she could barely remember the events. Yet when Patric had moved back into her life he'd almost taken it over.

And now he'd asked her to marry him.

Sinking down onto the bed, she stared at the floor. She would have to tell him who Nick's father was; she couldn't marry him with that lie still between them. She should have told him when he'd said he wanted a future with her, but she'd been a coward.

She could not marry Patric without telling him who her son's father was. To put it in Nick's terms, it simply wasn't fair. If he was the man she thought he was, he'd accept it.

If not—then she'd manage.

Starkly she thought she'd *have* to manage.

Tonight. She had to tell him tonight.

It would be all right, she comforted herself. Patric hadn't said that he loved her, but why else would he ask her to marry him? He'd forgive her for lying to him. And he'd make sure she never had to meet Sean again—from what Patric had said, even Sean's mother had given up on him. Poor Mrs Cusack. Perhaps she might find some sort of consolation with the children Kate had every intention of giving Patric.

Yes, she'd tell him tonight.

Ignoring a craven clutch of panic, Kate dried her hair and got into her clothes, wishing she had more of a choice. It would be wonderful to select from several gorgeous designer outfits, stunning and provocative and glamorous, but her wardrobe reflected her tight budget.

At least the garments in it now suited her. Until she'd started working in the shop she'd worn mostly secondhand clothes.

Patric arrived dead on time. 'I thought we'd eat at the house I'm staying in,' he said as they drove through the small city.

Normally he stayed in a hotel. Chilled by an odd sense of exclusion, she asked, 'Where is it?'

'The Heads.'

Whangarei lay at the tidal limit of a drowned river valley, its north bank a series of volcanoes forced millions of years previously through the earth's mantle. Long dead, they'd weathered into jagged, dramatic hills known as The Heads, their rock faces and sharp outlines a formidable hurdle for the sun each morning.

Tell him now, she urged herself, after he's negotiated this set of traffic lights.

But before she could speak he said, 'You'll meet Geoff and Suse Simpson one day, but at the moment they're in England. They offered me the house whenever I wanted to stay.'

'I already know Mrs Simpson as a customer.' Kate looked determinedly out of the side window. She'd wait until they got to the house. It would be easier to confess when he wasn't concentrating on the road. 'She's nice.' She didn't mention that the owner of the shop had made it clear that Mrs Simpson was important.

'I'm glad you like her,' Patric said. 'Geoff and I went to school together.'

Geoffrey Simpson was now a very successful solicitor, working in his father's practice. His wife ran a flying school and bought most of her very elegant clothes in Auckland and Australia.

Kate knew they lived in a lovely house; she discovered that it was truly fantastic, set high above the tidal estuary so that it looked south across Bream Bay to the Hen and Chicken Islands, and on to Great Barrier Island and its rugged inner companion, Little Barrier. Glittering, compelling, limitless, the sea dazzled to the horizon.

'Impressive,' Kate said, wishing she had more sophistication. Her nerves were jangling, and her voice sounded colourless. *Tell him now.*

'The house or the view?'

She turned away from the window to glance around the huge, exquisitely furnished sitting room. Her eyes lingered on a picture, all stark angles and bold juxtapositions of colour. It was exciting, almost alarming. 'Both.'

Coward!

Patric smiled at her. 'I'll get you a drink. What would you like?'

Grateful for the respite, she chose white wine; he poured her a fragrant Riesling, grown on the stony plains of Marlborough, and whisky and water for himself. Upright in a black leather Wassily chair, Kate sipped the superb wine and tried to forget her hollow foreboding.

'You're not thinking of going back on your promise this afternoon, I hope,' Patric said conversationally, watching her from heavy-lidded eyes.

Her hand jumped, almost spilling the wine. Carefully she set the glass down. 'I was wondering whether you were regretting having asked for it,' she said, pronouncing each word with circumspection. He hadn't touched her since he'd picked her up.

'You know better, Kate.' But his eyes were hooded, a formidable control keeping them blank.

In spite of the fine tremor in her hand she picked up the glass and swallowed a large mouthful of wine. 'Nick is still thrilled. I imagine he's telling the MacArthurs all about it right now.' *Now!*

But he asked without emphasis, 'What would you have said if Nick had hated the idea?' Before she could speak he said curtly, 'That's a stupid question. Forget it.'

She had to answer. 'I don't know. I'd have tried to change his mind.' And, because that seemed a cavilling response, she added, 'He admires you enormously.'

'Fortunately for me. So now,' the cool, dark voice prompted, 'I'd like to know what your problem is. Something's eating at you.'

Clutching the glass, she said, 'Patric—I need to tell you about Nick's father.'

The whisky glass rang as he set it down on the glass side table. 'No.'

Ignoble relief flooded through her, but she couldn't accept it. White-lipped, she stammered, 'I—I have to—'

'I don't want to hear.' His voice was inflexible, obdurate. 'I don't need to know anything more than you've already told me. It doesn't matter. I have everything I've ever wanted.'

Intent, his face under such rigid control it could have been carved in stone, he came across to her and pulled her gently to her feet. He didn't say anything; instead he held her close until the comfort only he could give her worked its magic. Her fears faded and shimmered into mirages, into nothingness.

'Kate,' he said eventually.

'What?'

'Just—Kate. My Kate. For ever this time.'

But he made no effort to kiss her. Bewildered, Kate looked up into narrowed, molten eyes, and realised with a jumping heartbeat that he was going to let her take the initiative. For a second memory intruded—a memory of rough hands and jeers, of helplessness and pain and degradation—and then it flickered and died.

This was Patric. She trusted him.

'I won't break,' she said, and stood on her toes so that she could touch her lips to his hard, beautiful mouth.

Time stretched, lingered. His lips were firm and totally unresponsive.

Kate was just about to jerk away when his arms contracted and he took her mouth in a kiss stripped of everything but passion and hunger. Vaguely she thought she sensed the second his self-control broke. It was followed almost immediately by the breaching of her own barriers; without any resistance she surrendered the guarded citadel of her body and her heart.

Sensation flooded through her. As she opened her lips beneath his she wondered vaguely how her response to Patric's mouth—to his scent and corded strength, his hands—flowed sweet and languorous as honey, yet at the same time pierced her with a sharp, swift ecstasy.

He broke the kiss to speak. 'Now do you understand

how I feel about you?' His voice was guttural as he fought
to master himself.

Suddenly shy, she nodded.

'Then I think we'd better stop,' he said thickly.

Bewildered, her head spinning, Kate asked, 'Why?'

He said, 'I won't rush you as I did last time.'

Her heart swelled. She didn't need to hear the words—
this was indication enough that he loved her. 'That was a
long time ago,' she said, tracing his straight mouth with
her fingertip. His lips were a little blurred by that fierce
kiss, and a trace of heat stained the high, autocratic cheekbones.

Kate's spine tingled into meltdown. In a voice that trembled, she continued, 'I'm not an eighteen-year-old girl
now, Patric.'

Half-closed, gleaming eyes held hers for so long that
her heartbeat surged into overdrive. The dense colour of
his pupils concealed his thoughts; as she waited for his
answer a remnant of practicality cooled her wildfire response. Although she had no protection, she'd more or less
invited him to make love to her.

And she still had to tell him.

Gathering her courage in her hands, she said huskily,
'Patric—darling—please listen to me. This is important.
Please—'

He bent and kissed the hollow beneath her ear. Mouth
moving with erotic finesse on her skin, he said, 'Hush. I
have no other personal commitments, Kate. Only to you
and to Nick.'

And before she had time to remind herself of the reason
they shouldn't make love yet, he kissed her again and she
yielded, helpless against the driving force of his sensuous
persuasion.

CHAPTER TEN

MAKING love with Patric was like being engulfed by a hurricane—no, like submitting to the powerful, remorseless surge of the ocean, becoming one with it. On a shuddering sigh Kate surrendered to his skilled hands, to his clever, experienced mouth, to the feverish drumming of her hunger.

How did he know that her breasts ached for the touch of his hands? When he slid his hand up under the lining of her singlet top she sighed with relief, and arched so that he could reach her more easily.

'Motherhood suits you,' he said, his voice raw as he cupped the slight curves.

Sensation shimmered through her, wild and turbulent as the sea, speeding from the skin beneath his hands to every hidden, waiting part.

Stunned, her body aflame, Kate turned her face into his throat. Delicately she tasted him again, delighting in the flavour that was Patric—as much the man as the iron-blue sheen of his eyes, the determined, confident mouth that held such heaven.

'Have you changed too?' she asked against his neck.

'Why don't you find out?' he suggested tautly. 'But not here.'

With one swift, easy movement he scooped her up and carried her along the high white hall and into a bedroom cantilevered over the hillside, suspended between the sky and the sea. Through huge windows Kate saw the moon rising, following a white moonpath across the black waters, silhouetting the stark, unambiguous shapes of the extinct volcanoes against a sky robbed of all but the brightest stars.

Patric put her down on the bed. As he pulled the ribbon free from her hair and lifted the clinging tresses so that he could kiss her nape, he asked in a tight, disciplined voice, 'Do you want me to draw the curtains?'

Almost seven years ago they'd made love in his parents' house, in the bedroom he'd slept in since a child. Curtains had covered the windows and the room had seemed a safe haven, a nest. But that wasn't what she wanted now.

'No.'

Without moving he said, 'Kate, I've got protection.'

Almost inaudibly she said, 'Patric, that's up to you. I want to give you a child.'

Blue flames in his eyes swallowed the darkness. He spread a handful of her hair across her throat, then kissed the vulnerable hollow where her pulse beat fast and high.

'I used to dream of this,' he said in a quiet, almost soundless voice. 'Of you with the moon on your face and that hair spread on my pillows, and your smile for me only. Kate, if I'd known—'

'But you didn't,' she interrupted, desperate that their coming together not be overshadowed by the past. Wary of the dimness that obscured the future, she felt secure only in this rich, glorious present. 'Patric, it's over now. The past's gone—done with, finished. We're together again.'

Raising lazy, boneless hands, she undid the top button of his shirt and then the next, her senses thrilling as his chest lifted on a sharply indrawn breath. Words lingered drowsily on her tongue. 'We've got this, and each other, and Nick—so much, my darling, so much. Isn't that enough?'

Without waiting for an answer, she kissed the skin she'd uncovered, rejoicing as his heart thundered beneath her lips. 'Patric,' she whispered, and pulled his shirt free. 'I need you so much.'

The moon's restrained light silvered the broad shoulders

that tapered to narrow waist and hips, revealed the flexion of the long muscles in his arms when he pulled her singlet top over her head and looked at her with dark, flat eyes—eyes that devoured her with the same craving that ate into her heart.

That was the moment she really believed.

'Kate,' he said through lips that barely moved. 'Kate—it's so banal to say that you're beautiful, but it's the only thing I can say. You steal my strength, scramble my brain, reduce me to a mindless collection of driving hungers, and yet I've never wanted any other woman so much.'

Leaning forward, she kissed along the line of his shoulder, feeling the skin tighten, kindle beneath her questing mouth. 'Darling,' she breathed.

'I've spent nearly seven years starving for you,' he said, his voice ragged with emotion he no longer tried to hide. 'Wherever I've been, whatever I've been doing, I've looked for you, because without you I was only half a man. You were so young, and yet you gave yourself utterly, generously. And you demanded the same from me—everything. At twenty-four I rather prided myself on my understanding of women—thought I knew what passion was all about; you showed me that it was nothing without love.'

Kate whispered, 'I know. I know, Patric. But we're together now. We don't have to hide any more.'

Deliberately, worshipfully, like participants in some ancient ceremony older than time, they looked at each other. Kate's heart lurched as she drowned in the depths of Patric's eyes.

'Sometimes I wondered if I'd dreamed you,' he said hoarsely. 'Nobody could be so sweet and sensual, so gentle yet excitingly, elementally demanding. Night after night, year after year, you've haunted me, and each time I woke to loneliness.'

Shaken, her eyes dilated, she returned, 'I understand loneliness.'

His features hardening into a bronze mask, he pulled her up and measured her waist with his hands for a breathless second before sliding them up again to cup her naked breasts. Kate shivered at the strength of his long fingers.

'Yes,' Patric said unevenly. His lips drew back in a humourless smile, and he bent his head and suckled her.

Sensation splintered through her like lightning, shattering the last remnants of her will. Her strange, wild cry echoed desolately in the silent room, as the insistent heat and tug of his mouth quickened every cell in her body.

Groaning, he lifted her to meet the demands of his avid mouth.

Inside her, struggling through the languidly erotic sensations aroused by his mouth, some darker, more urgent need began to demand fulfilment. The strength and power of his arousal summoned a primitive desire; she shivered as her feet touched the floor.

'What is it?' he asked, his voice stripped of everything but raw need.

'Just you.'

His eyes searched hers. All barriers surrendered, Kate flattened her hand over his heart and smiled at the sudden thunder beneath her palm.

'Siren,' he said on an impeded breath.

Leaning forward, Kate kissed one of the small male nipples. She measured it with her teeth, softly biting, then kissed it again. Exhilaration coursed through her when he shuddered.

'Yes,' he said, as though she'd asked a question.

Deftly he removed the sage-green trousers and the skin-coloured briefs beneath. A moment later cotton sheets cooled her as she watched the man she loved kick off the rest of his clothes and lie down beside her on the bed.

All those years ago he had been tender, gentle, his love-making a salute to her youth and innocence.

Not now. Compelled by a desire he could no longer curb, Patric made love with a fierce, wildly erotic concentration, taking Kate into realms of the senses she'd only read about.

Confidence flowered in her, because at last she knew Sean's violence hadn't frozen her natural appetite. Urged on by a taut, receptive impatience, she went with Patric into that place where the only reality was his hands and his mouth and the sound of their hearts beating above the voluptuous clamour of her body, where thought was replaced by instinct, where the slow slide of his mouth across her hipbone was worth more than all the pearls in the sea, all the security in the world.

Patric turned his head to kiss the satiny top of her thigh. His hair brushed against her, the rasp of his shaven cheek quivering through her acutely susceptible body. Without volition she lifted herself against him in silent, insistent demand.

'Not yet,' he said huskily. 'Not yet, Kate.'

But that aching torment demanded satisfaction. Drugged by delight, she'd been lying in a kind of stunned stasis; now, without haste, she ran her hands from his chest down the flat muscles of his stomach, following the line of hair that pointed the way. Her teeth found the smooth swell of muscle across his shoulder; she bit into the heated skin, then licked the small abrasion.

He muttered, 'No,' and trapped her exploring fingers in a peremptory hand.

She lifted heavy eyelids. Hunger—dominating, uncompromising—emphasised the stark framework of his face. Dark, half-closed eyes glittered; his mouth was curved in a smile that owed nothing to amusement.

An instinct old as womanhood—an inborn understanding of seduction—stirred in Kate. Clasping her hands across his back, she arched up onto his strong shaft and began to pull herself around him, enclosing him, her muscles working to embed him in the silken channel that longed for him.

Her name erupted in a predatory, goaded monosyllable,

then he surged into her, the power of his whole body behind the compulsive initial thrust.

He filled her so completely that although his caresses
had ensured the softening and moisture needed to ease his
entrance, she took a sharp, involuntary breath.

He said through gritted teeth, 'Kate?'

'Oh, yes,' she answered on a sigh.

Almost tentatively she clenched her inner muscles and
he grated, 'Yes, like that, like that...' and began to move.

Kate's hands fastened around his shoulders, the slick,
hot skin delighting her fingertips until she forgot everything but the urgent rhythm of Patric's lovemaking and her
own wild response. She came apart in his arms, unravelling
in a consuming tide of desire.

Gradually, inexorably, sensation heightened, intensified,
gripping her in fiery bonds. Consumed by ripples of pleasure, she began to strive towards some unknown apex of
experience, her body tightening as she met his thrusts and
matched them.

The ripples expanded, drowning her in pleasure; gasping
his name, Kate forced her eyes open, trying to find some
stable point in this maelstrom of passion. He was watching
her, that humourless smile etched against his face, and as
she was flung deep, deep down, as the light rushed over
her, as waves of rapture spun her into some other dimen-
sion, he came with her, head flung back, his voice echoing
in her ears while she fell into ecstasy.

How long it lasted she never knew. Not long enough,
and yet any more could have tipped her over the edge into
madness.

Aftershocks still shivered through Kate as slow, merciless reality pushed its way back into the enclosure of their
love. Helpless tears ached behind her eyes.

Still breathing heavily, his voice guttural and strained,
Patric said, 'I hurt you.'

'I'm all right.'

But he moved over onto his side and scooped her to

face him, the dark eyes intent as they searched her face. 'What is it?' he demanded. 'How much did it hurt?'

'It didn't.' Nothing would ever hurt her again; he'd just stolen her heart from her body and banished, with his skilful, urgent, wholehearted passion, the memories of Sean's attack, finally and conclusively healing an injury she'd thought long mended.

She struggled to achieve a watery smile. 'I didn't know it could be like that,' she said, the words so filled with wonder that his expression relaxed. She turned her face into his chest, and Patric lifted a hand to quietly, rhythmically, stroke her hair.

'Neither did I,' he said, and into his voice came a sombre note. 'A total, complete submersion that for precious, unbearable moments makes me whole.'

'Yes.' Her voice trembled.

All these years, she thought dizzily, she'd been walking around in an emotional shroud. Cut off from the sensual pleasures of physical contact, she'd thought she was safe.

Patric had ripped her cloak of numbness from her, leaving her at the mercy of this ravishment that robbed her of the ability to think, to do anything other than feel. He had restored her to herself, made her whole again.

They drove home through a fresh, glistening dawn, bright, sun-sprinkled, poised on the border of spring and summer.

At the town basin they stopped to drink coffee and eat fresh-baked rolls. Neither said much. Relaxed, although her muscles protested now and then, Kate could only look at Patric, her mouth still tender from his kisses, her heart so full no words seemed adequate.

Inserting the key into her door, he said, 'I have to go to Australia this afternoon, but I'll be home on Wednesday— I'll come up then and we'll make plans. Until then—keep safe, my darling. You hold my heart in your keeping.' He bent and dropped a quick, hard kiss on her lips. 'And give your notice in at the shop,' he instructed.

The sun gleamed blue-black on his head, across the skin she'd kissed the night before. 'Yes, sir,' Kate said smartly.

His brows shot up. 'Did I sound too autocratic? Blame the way you look at me—as though I'm the sum of your hopes. It makes me feel like a king.' When Kate blushed he laughed, low and tender, with a note of passion beneath the amusement. 'Stop that or I'll never get away. Miss me.'

'Of course I'll miss you,' she said, resisting the temptation to cling. 'Travel safely, and come back to me.'

'Nothing,' he said, making the words a vow, '*nothing* will keep me from you. I swear it.'

She watched him stride down the path and get into the car. He lifted a hand and drove away, the big vehicle purring down the suburban street.

Hugging herself, so happy she couldn't bear it, Kate floated inside. In the small mirror in the bathroom she thought she saw her dreams dancing around her in a golden haze, drawing her along into a future she had never hoped for.

There'd be a period of adjustment; Patric still saw her as the schoolgirl—innocent and untouched—he'd once known. But they'd deal with it. A smile curved her lips; last night had begun that process! There was nothing they couldn't do together. And he was already on the way to loving Nick for himself, with the kind of solid love that nothing could jeopardise.

Nothing but Sean.

Appalled, her smile dying, she stared at her reflection. Making love to Patric had driven everything from her mind—she hadn't even thought about telling him after that. This incandescent happiness was built on a lie.

She should have insisted on revealing the truth before they made love, before they took the chance that might lead to another child. Now she'd have to wait until he came home from Australia, because there was no way she'd blurt it out over the telephone. Guilt plucked at her as she turned the water on and undressed.

At nine, she picked Nick up, refusing a cup of coffee with Ngaire, who was still wandering gloomily around in her dressing gown.

'Not that I have time to drink coffee, I suppose, if I'm going to get to church,' Ngaire grumbled. 'Nick was fine. And I don't need to ask if you had a good time—you look like someone who's just discovered the meaning of life.'

Kate blushed, ready to tell her, then closed her mouth on the words. Patric might reject—no, of course he wouldn't.

Her friend grinned. 'Oho! All right, I won't ask, but I want to know all the details when you're ready to tell me.' Slyly she added, 'Nick said your Patric is going to be his new father.'

'We've got a few things to straighten out first,' Kate said, longing to tell her, furious with herself for not confessing when she'd had the chance.

Ngaire laughed. 'I hope it works out for you, girl. You deserve to be happy.'

They'd barely got out of the gate before Nick demanded, 'Where is he? Where's Mr Sutherland—Dad?'

Kate explained.

'He didn't tell me,' he said, scowling to hide his hurt.

'He didn't tell me until this morning, either. He has work to do in Australia.'

'I thought he was going to be my father and live with us,' Nick said.

'We'll be living with him in Auckland, but you know fathers don't stay at home all the time. Mr MacArthur goes off to work.'

'Yes, but not on the weekend,' Nick protested.

'Mr MacArthur works in an office. Patric has to travel a lot, and that means he can't always stay home.'

Stubbornly he reiterated, 'He should've told me.'

Although rather silent for the rest of the day, Nick woke up the next morning his usual sunny self, and set off for school chattering about swimming and his ambition to dive.

Monday passed in a kind of a daze for Kate. She knew she was happy, yet she couldn't feel that essential lightness, an inner conviction. A life with Patric and Nick was spread before her, the gold of bliss woven through with crimson threads of passion, but she stood like an impostor before it. So much to look forward to, yet she was unable to believe it—because she hadn't told Patric the one thing he should know.

He rang that night from Australia.

'Is everything all right?' Kate asked, eyeing Nick who was hopping up and down impatiently.

'Why?'

'You sound tired.'

He paused, before telling her drily, 'I'm clearing up a mess of Sean's.'

The name was like a foul miasma. 'Oh,' she said over a sick foreboding. 'I thought you didn't see him?'

'I don't.' Patric allowed a note of exasperation to show. 'It's under control. Normally I wouldn't have anything to do with him, but his mother asked me to tidy this up. I hadn't realised they still keep in contact—but at least Aunt Barbara has the sense not to welcome him back into the fold. And I have to do this—he's been using my name.' Abruptly he changed the subject. 'Is Nick there?'

'Yes.' And because she felt ill she asked, 'Would you like to say hello?'

'Very much.'

Handing over the receiver, Kate poured herself a glass of water. The tightness in her throat eased when she drank it, but sudden, unexpected terror still smirched her happiness.

After several minutes Nick said importantly, 'All right, I'll get her.' He held the receiver out. 'He wants to talk to you,' he informed her unnecessarily.

Patric said, 'Kate, I have to go now. I'll try to ring you

again this time tomorrow night, so I can talk to Nick as well, but I'll see you on Wednesday anyway.' He stopped, and she could hear voices in the room with him. Quickly he finished, 'Take care.'

'You too,' she said, and replaced the receiver, cross with whoever had interrupted because they'd denied her a proper farewell.

Her pulse-rate was soon back to normal, though it took a while for the lingering nausea to clear. She was overreacting. Sean couldn't harm her or Nick.

But this time she'd tell Patric whether he wanted to hear or not.

Tense, worried, she waited until Patric rang again on Tuesday night, a hurried, unsatisfactory call this time that left her even more restless than ever.

Wooing sleep, she picked up a library book and tried to read. The words danced before her eyes, mocking her. Eventually she closed the book and looked around her bedroom. It was small, as were all the rooms in the unit, and the wallpaper had faded in the harsh Northland sun so that each tiny sprig of flowers looked like a dagger pointing downwards. The curtains were ones she'd made when she first came to Whangarei; her inexperience showed in puckered hems and uneven lengths, but she'd never been able to afford to replace them.

When she was with Patric she was sure they could overcome anything Fate threw in their path. Now, in her own surroundings, the cheap bedspread and secondhand furniture ample evidence of her poverty, she was afraid. She didn't know how to be a wife to someone like Patric. Oh, she was excellent mistress material, but a *wife*—she had never presided at a dinner party in her life! She had nothing in common with the sophisticated people he moved among. She probably wouldn't even like them.

His mother wouldn't welcome her.

And there was always Sean. And Patric's response to the truth.

Kate didn't sleep that night.

The following day she had to work until four-thirty, so Nick went home with Rangi after school. As she drove into the carport she thought that if—no, *when*—when she lived in Auckland she'd miss Ngaire very much, but Whangarei was only two hours away—they'd be able to see each other frequently.

Arms filled with bags of groceries, she set off for the back door.

Once inside she began to sort and store their contents, trying to enjoy the sound of a lovesick thrush coming through the open door. The day was cool and cloudy, with drizzly showers wafting between the hills, and every bird in Whangarei seemed to have caught the mating urge.

She never knew what made her realise she wasn't alone—perhaps some alteration in the texture of the air, or some hidden instinct warning her of danger. If so, it came far too late. By the time she'd turned towards the open back door Sean Cusack was inside.

Fear kicked in her stomach, stimulating a rush of adrenalin. Without thinking, she yanked out the kitchen drawer and snatched up her carving knife. 'If you come any further I'll see what damage I can do with this,' she said hoarsely.

'Oh, brave girl,' he jeered, his large, too-pale eyes salaciously flicking the length of her body, 'but you don't have to worry—I'm not going to touch you.'

'Get out.' Thank God Nick was at the MacArthurs'.

'Is that a nice way to greet a member of the family?' he drawled. 'God, I laughed when I realised my noble cousin was seeing you again. You should be careful when you talk on telephones, you know—there's always the possibility someone might be listening on an extension! Naturally, I hopped onto a plane and followed Patric home, all eagerness to find out exactly what was going on. My poor, silly mother told me he'd been paying a lot of visits to Whangarei, so I looked you up, and there you were in the phone book! Does Patric know that your brat could be mine?'

Stone-faced, Kate held the knife in front of her, but he must have seen something in her expression because he gave a long, soft whistle and the handsome, fleshy face crumpled into laughter.

'He *is* mine, isn't he? And you've told Patric he's his. I should have stuck with you, pretty Kate—you certainly know how to organise things to your advantage.'

'Get out,' she said steadily.

'Not on your life, darling.' His voice was gleeful. 'So he doesn't know that you slept with me.'

'You can be thankful that he *doesn't* know you raped me,' she said evenly.

A momentary unease drained some of the colour from his skin. 'You wanted it,' he said viciously. 'You loved it—you only kicked up a fuss because you thought he might marry you, and you knew I had no money.'

Her skin crawled. 'You raped me,' she repeated, watching him intently, determined to make sure he never touched her again.

'Try telling my cousin that and see if he believes you. He's always been jealous because I'm better-looking than him. Anyway,' he sneered, 'it wasn't as if you were a virgin.'

This man couldn't hurt her—she wasn't even afraid of him. All he'd had of her was the unwilling use of her body. His brutality hadn't even been directed at her—he'd raped her because she was Patric's lover; it was Patric he hated and envied, and it was Patric and Nick she had to protect.

'Anyway, he doesn't care about you,' he said, the words bursting bitterly from him. 'He thinks the kid's his—that's why he's marrying you. Once you're hitched he'll ignore you just like he did Laura.'

'Go away, Sean,' Kate said with disdain. 'You can't make any more trouble. You're nothing.'

Scarlet-faced, he stared belligerently at her. Then he caught himself up; his colour faded, and the glitter in his eyes transmuted into calculation. Incredulously, she realised that he was laughing.

'Oh, this is rich. This is brilliantly rich. My arrogant, stuck-up cousin will just hate bringing up another man's bastard—especially mine,' he said, gasping with enjoyment. 'You know, I think—I really think—that it's my cousinly duty to tell Patric. What a shame. We'll see how high he holds his head up then.'

'Tell him if you dare,' she said icily. 'And he already knows my son is not his.'

'Oh, I dare. After all, it only comes down to your word against mine—and he's not trusting where women are concerned, whereas I'm family.'

Even though he was threatening her, Kate could discern his pathetic pride in being related to the Sutherlands. 'Why would he believe your lies? As for my son—Patric knows he isn't his,' Kate repeated bluntly.

'Of course, if I tell him that will put an end to your little scheme to marry well.' Sean was watching her eagerly, slyness marring his regular features. 'However, it would give me great pleasure to watch him acting as father to my son, so perhaps I won't tell him just yet.' He paused, heavily underscoring his next words. 'If you make it worth my while not to.'

'Pay you off?' She didn't try to hide her disgust. 'You must be mad.'

Anger flamed in his eyes. 'No, you snooty-faced little bitch, I'm not mad. If you want to keep your hands on my big cousin and his spectacular bank account you can bloody well pay me.'

Lip curling, she said, 'I have no money.'

He flung back his head and laughed. 'I can get all the money I need from Patric—he has this stupid sense of family honour. But money isn't the only way to pay off a man, you know. I enjoyed our interlude together last time—I'd enjoy taking you to bed even more if you were Patric's wife. Especially as I know you'd hate it. Just what sacrifices are you prepared to make for your son, Kate?'

Kate masked her agony with burning disdain. 'I wouldn't sleep—' she said, then cried out, for Patric came through the door and she saw murder in his face.

Sean swung around. His swaggering bravado left him, crumpling before the black fury in Patric's eyes.

'No!' Kate shouted, dropping the knife and racing forward.

With terrifying speed and ferocity Patric hit Sean in the mouth, and then again, seeming not to realise that Kate was clinging to his arm, pleading, 'No, Patric, no, no, no,' as Sean fell backwards across the floor and lay still, blood trickling from a cut lip.

Patric's eyes were polished and fathomless, wiped clean of emotion. Fighting down her despair, Kate managed to say clearly, 'He's not worth it. He's trash, rubbish, a nothing. He's not worth it, Patric.'

Very gently he put her aside. 'Get up,' he said to his cousin, controlled menace icing each word.

Sean scrambled to his feet and backed up against the bench. His eyes darted from Patric's implacable face to Kate's and back again. He didn't speak.

In a quiet, conversational tone, Patric said, 'Get out of here and don't ever come back. If I see you within a hundred miles of Kate or the boy I'll have you put in prison for stalking.'

Sean waited until he was well out of the door before shouting, 'I hope you enjoy bringing up my son, Patric.'

Kate forced breath into her aching lungs, closed for a second the eyes that were stretched too wide.

'Why didn't you tell me?' Patric asked with deadly composure.

'At first I couldn't bear to. I knew you despised him, and for some reason it was—it was worse that it was Sean, and not some anonymous, dead rapist.' Her voice sounded

thin, remote. She waited, and when he said nothing she
went on without hope, 'It made it personal. I'm not making
sense, am I? But that's how I felt, and I hoped...'

'What did you hope? That you'd never have to tell me?'

She searched his face, but saw nothing there to give her
confidence. In an exhausted voice she said, 'Yes. You
said...you said you never saw Sean, so I thought Nick was
safe.' And, knowing he wouldn't believe her, she added,
'When you asked me to marry you, I knew I'd have to tell
you, but I didn't know how you'd react. I was a coward.'
She hadn't known it then, but she hadn't trusted him
enough. Lamely, she finished, 'I did try, but when you said
you didn't want to know I was relieved and glad. I should
have insisted on telling you then. I'm so sorry, Patric.'

Patric looked down at his bruised knuckles, stained with
the blood from Sean's split lip. Numbly Kate turned the
tap on over the sink and handed him a paper towel. When
he'd washed his hands and wiped the water from them he
flexed the long fingers.

Kate asked, 'Was he right? Did you think I was lying—
that Nick is yours?'

He met her pleading glance with unreadable self-
possession. 'At first, yes,' he said. 'The day I met you
again I rang New Zealand and got someone to check his
birth certificate. You didn't put the name of his father, but
you called him Nicholas Patrick. And he reminded me so
much of the way I was as a kid—as ''Black'' Pat used to
be—his almost obsessive interests, even the way he tilted
his head. Of course I thought he was mine.'

Her heart broke. Kate felt it quite clearly, shuddered at
the sudden rending, the agonising pain as her hopes shattered, each jagged shard cutting her into shreds. She'd lied,
but so had he—he had pursued her because he wanted the
boy he'd thought was his son. 'I called him after you because I wanted to give him something of you,' she whispered shakily. 'It was all I had, all I could do for him. But
it was a lie.'

Still speaking with that rigid, dispassionate composure, he went on, 'And you didn't seem very upset when you told me about being raped. In fact you were very calm.'

White-lipped, her voice barely under control, she said, 'Apart from a therapist, you're the first person I've ever told. The only way I could say the words was to cut myself off from any emotion.'

He swore—raw words delivered in a flat monotone—and then fell silent. Even when he spoke again he made no movement towards her, didn't touch her. 'I never know what you're thinking, how you feel.'

Anger splintered through her, eating up the adrenalin. She shouted, 'Why would I have made up a story about being raped?'

'To punish me for marrying Laura.' Suddenly, he smashed his maltreated hand onto the bench. Kate's breath hissed through her lips as he said evenly, 'I should have known—God, I should have seen that there was something fundamentally wrong with you at that last meeting in May when you told me you didn't love me any more! I was so lost in my own problems, it never occurred to me that...'

To her horror she saw that his eyes were wet.

She exclaimed, 'No! How could you? I made sure you didn't! I tried so hard to seem normal—and you were under such pressure yourself. Patric, don't blame yourself.'

He said savagely, 'I'll blame myself until the day I die.'

Her fury collapsed into dread. 'When did you realise that I'd told you the truth in Surfers' Paradise—that Nick isn't your son?'

'I realised you *had* been raped when I drove you up to the Bay of Islands for dinner. You said so simply that you couldn't marry me when you were carrying another man's child.'

She remembered then—that glimpse of his face in the headlights, the way he'd forgotten to dip the car lights.

'But I didn't know the rapist was my cousin, another descendant of ''Black'' Pat, so I still believed Nick was mine.' He spoke without inflection. 'There's a photograph of ''Black'' Pat taken when he was five in an old album— they could be twins. I thought that some miracle had made Nick mine.'

Pain squeezed Kate's heart, dimmed her vision.

'I felt murderous—and ashamed,' Patric continued almost soundlessly. 'I was bitterly glad that the man who'd done that to you was dead. And I knew that I had to go very gently with you, that you might still distrust men— that you might never be able to want me as I wanted you.' Some emotion broke through the bronze mask of his face. 'Why didn't you tell me when we met that last time at Tatamoa? Surely you didn't think I'd discard you because Sean raped you?'

Past weariness, Kate leaned back against the counter. She wanted him to go before she abandoned herself to grief at the destruction of all those shining golden hopes, but she owed him an explanation. 'I went into a deep depression and I wasn't thinking at all straight. I knew you despised him and—I felt dirty, demeaned, no fit woman for you. I was sure you'd never accept his child. Your father was dying; if I'd told you you'd have confronted Sean, and it would have ripped your family apart. In the end it was all too much. I loved you, but I wanted to get away, to be free of everything that had happened.'

His mouth twisted. 'He raped you because you were mine, because he hated me. He went around with a smirk for months, and I didn't realise—it barely bloody registered! And I still didn't realise when you told me about it. How can you forgive me for such blindness?'

Tensely, urgently she said, 'There's no question of forgiving you, of blaming you. I can imagine how hideous those months must have been for you. Anyway, Sean's sins are his, not yours.'

Patric said quietly, 'You're infinitely more forgiving than I am. I'd like to kill him.'

'I was afraid of that,' she said quietly.

'Is that why you didn't tell me?'

She flushed at the incredulity in his tone. 'Partly.'

'I'm not a murderer, Kate.'

'I know,' she said quickly, 'but you—I didn't know how you'd react! *Why* does he hate you so much?'

He looked past her, his expression bleak. 'Sean feels that because Aunt Barbara was older than my father she should have inherited half of Sutherland Aviation, and probably he's right, but ''Black'' Pat was an unregenerate chauvinist and so was my father. Instead of a share in the business she got a trust fund which her husband persuaded her to waste on speculations that invariably came to nothing.'

There was more to it than that, Kate thought, her anger dying and leaving her hollow, emptied out of emotion. Sean hated Patric because he was everything Sean was not.

Still in that distant, deadly voice, Patric said, 'I put up with Sean for years, but when he tried to blackmail his mother into handing over money from the new trust fund I'd set up for her it was too much. You'll never see him again.'

Exhausted, Kate said, 'But he's still Nick's father— nothing can alter that. I think you'd better go now.'

'Kate—'

She couldn't bear to listen. 'Patric, please go,' she said wearily.

He had betrayed her as she had betrayed him; he'd courted her to claim the boy he'd believed to be his son.

'Kate, I can't leave you now,' he said urgently. 'I can't abandon you—'

Something snapped inside her. Summoning every atom of strength and determination she possessed, she said, 'You are not abandoning me; you didn't abandon me all those years ago. I'm now a grown woman, and at the moment I need to learn to cope with the fact that you deliberately pursued me to get your hands on a child you believed to be yours. I need to be alone to do that, Patric.'

'All right,' he said between his teeth. 'I have things I need to face too, but I'll be back. I'm at the hotel. If Sean tries to contact you again, ring me there.' He looked at her, the dark eyes turbulent and angry. In a hard voice he finished, 'If you need me, ring me. I'll come, Kate—you only have to call and I'll come.'

It wasn't until Nick had gone to bed that Kate was able to sit down and face what had happened. Pain ached through her heart, clogged the back of her throat, throbbed in her head. If only she hadn't succumbed to the temptation to give her son Patrick for a second name she'd probably have convinced Patric right at the start that she'd been raped, and he'd have left them alone.

Was there any hope for them?

Don't give in, she thought grimly. You've dealt with pain before and survived. You can do it again.

But this was something more than pain—this was the defilement of her hopes and illusions, a keen agony she'd never escape even though the years might smooth over the raw edges of the scar.

When the telephone rang she was tempted to ignore it, but the possibility that it might be Patric galvanised her to her feet.

'I thought you might like to know,' came Sean's hateful, gloating voice, 'that I'm applying to the courts tomorrow for access to the brat. I think it's time I got to know my son—taught him a few things.'

Numb with horror, Kate slammed the receiver down and crept back to the sofa, pleating a corner of the throw with shaking fingers while her thoughts whirled in jumbled, terrified fragments around her head.

Eventually, however, her movements stilled. Abruptly she sat up and straightened her shoulders. 'No!' she exclaimed to a silent room.

Sean would never get his greedy, corrupt hands on Nick. Never. If he persisted she'd deny everything. DNA testing would be the only way anyone would be able to tell for certain who Nick's father was. And if Sean suggested that she'd make plans to run—

The telephone burst into her plotting. Stiffly she rose to pick it up and spat, 'You come anywhere near him and I'll be at the police station tomorrow morning accusing you of rape.' Lying, she added, 'My aunt will give evidence. I told her at the time. I mean it, Sean.'

There was a second of silence before Patric said in a low, furious voice, 'I'll be up straight away.'

Patric arrived within ten minutes. He looked just the same, except for a feral danger in his eyes she'd not seen before.

'Tell me exactly what he said,' he commanded as soon as he got there.

Word for word she repeated Sean's threat.

'He's trying to bluff you,' he said, then shook his head. 'No, it's me. He's blackmailing me. He'll demand financial support in return for not going ahead with it.'

Kate said, 'But how can he believe you'd give in?'

He gave her a hard, ironic smile. 'He knows me well,' he said. 'He knows that I'd do anything in the world for you.'

In a cracked, unsteady voice she said, 'Patric, please don't. At least you didn't lie before. Don't lie now.'

After a second's hesitation, he said quietly, 'I didn't realise it, but I wanted you to admit that you loved me before I told you how much I love you. Perhaps it was a petty revenge for not marrying me all those years ago. I hope not. If it was I've been punished, because you haven't said it.'

Kate plopped down on the sofa, huddling into the throw rug. Colour burned through her skin. 'You must know how I feel about you.'

'I know I can make you want me,' he said roughly, 'but it's not enough, Kate. You see, I've always loved you. I never lost hope that one day I'd find you again. In fact I knew I would, because you're the only reason I breathe. Yes, I was sure Nick was mine, and at first I thought I was cold-bloodedly pursuing you for my son, but it only took a few days for me to realise that nothing had changed. I didn't care whether you were lying or not—it didn't matter. I've never stopped loving you, and I never will.'

It was impossible not to believe him; the truth was stark, non-negotiable—in his tone, in the autocratic features clenched in intolerable emotion, in the dark, uncompromising eyes.

Transfixed by the stripped, aching need she saw there, Kate whispered, 'Patric, I love you so much I can't bear to think of exposing you to Sean's malice.'

'I can deal with him.' His tone sent shivers the length of her spine. 'I'm finding it very difficult to deal with the knowledge that Sean abused you because you were *my* lover. You were raped, forced to endure such degradation, because I loved you.'

She said succinctly, 'And because I made him look a fool when he tried to kiss me. Remember, I hit him in the solar plexus. He hated that.'

'It was my love that brought you horror and pain and years of loneliness. I left you this afternoon because I needed to be absolutely sure that I could still love Nick knowing he's Sean's, because I know you won't marry me without being convinced I'd make him happy.'

A bubble of emotion stopped her breath.

He walked across the room and took her hand carefully, smoothing away its tension. Dark, intense, his eyes held hers as he said, 'I *am* sure. I can never right the wrong that Sean did to you and I'll carry that guilt all my life, but I love his son, Kate, for a whole variety of reasons: because he's yours, of course, but most of all for what he is—a charming, interesting, lovable, strong-minded little boy, a son any man would be proud of. I'll be a good father to him, and to any other children we have. And I swear I'll try to be the best husband for you.'

Over the huge lump in her throat, she whispered, 'I love you.'

It was surrender and he knew it. His smile was tender and triumphant and relieved, as though he hadn't been sure.

Lifting her, he sat with her on the sofa. Cradled in the strong haven of his arms, Kate drew a deep breath and turned her face against his chest.

'Patric, I meant what I said before. You mustn't blame yourself for Sean's actions, because nobody but Sean is responsible for them.'

'You're too generous.'

His revulsion and remorse could be a problem. 'Oh, well, agonise, then,' she retorted. 'Perhaps you should never go anywhere near a woman in case your wicked cousin rapes her.'

After a moment's startled silence, he laughed with a note of genuine amusement. 'You're good for me,' he said, kissing the top of her head.

'And you are good for me. Don't ever forget that, Patric.' She hesitated, then said quietly, 'Your mother's not going to be happy about us.'

His answer was blunt. 'You're certainly not the wife she'd choose for me, but believe me, my darling, she's learned her lesson. She wants grandchildren and to see me happily married, not necessarily in that order.' He tipped her head and looked at her with gleaming, narrowed eyes. 'Being married to you will make me happy.'

'We'll keep each other happy,' she said, determined to enlist his mother's support and learn how to be the very best wife she could be for Patric.

He dropped a swift, scorching kiss on her mouth, and said, 'Trust me, Kate. We'll make it.'

'I do trust you.'

His unsparing eyes searched her face. 'Yes, I think you do, at last,' he said, and his arms tightened around her in a brief, fierce hug. 'I trust you, too.'

Dreamily, Kate thought she'd remember that precious moment all her life.

He said, 'We'll get married in three days' time. And we'll get DNA-tested. After I left you this afternoon I rang a friend of my father's to find out how it works, and apparently there could be enough similarity between Sean's test and mine to confuse the issue. So if Sean does press for access we can wave the results around the courtroom. Also, I have several other documents he won't want published; they'd ensure that no judge would grant access.'

'If he makes any move at all,' Kate said, shocked by the vindictiveness in her voice, 'I'll accuse him of rape. It will be awful, and I know your aunt will hate me for it, but I'll do it.'

'You won't have to. If he shows his face in New Zealand again I'll crush him.' It was said with such icy dispassion that she shivered. Instantly he demanded, 'Does he frighten you?'

'No,' she said contemptuously. 'Sex is nothing when it's stolen and forced. He wanted to humiliate and shame us both, but it would be giving him too much power to let him succeed. Actually, meeting him again helped me. I realised what a contemptible thing he is. But I do worry about Nick. I don't ever want him to know that Sean is his father.'

'We'll make sure he never does,' Patric said with lethal menace. 'I can control Sean. Our best revenge will be bringing up a son who is happy and successful and honest, and you've made a very good start on that. Between us we can make sure that Nick is nothing like the man who fathered him.'

He lifted her chin and looked at her, his hard face at last open to her. 'So now,' he said, 'may I stay the night with you, my darling? I need to hold you and make sure you're safe.'

Her eyes filled; nodding, she got up with him and went

into the bedroom, not worrying in the least that it was furnished with cast-offs.

This had nothing of the edged urgency of their last coming together; Patric undressed her slowly and sensuously, telling her how beautiful she was to him, how he ached for her, what he planned to do, how he hoped she'd feel.

Kate did the same for him, and when at last they lay together in bed she thought that this was how it had been the first time—profoundly, heart-stoppingly tender.

Although she'd been much shyer then, and Patric hadn't complained about the bed!

'Just as well I've got a decent-sized one at home,' he grumbled as they lay heart to heart, her face pressed into his neck, her body singing with anticipation. 'We won't live in the apartment—I want to buy you a house by the sea.'

Kate laughed silently, and ran a questing hand down the indentation of his spine and across to his hip. Her whole world, she thought exultantly, was blooming like a garden in spring.

A garden with a snake, but she trusted Patric to deal with his cousin.

'You don't need to make love if you don't want to,' Patric said, although his chest lifted suddenly at her caress. 'I meant it when I told you it would be enough to hold you.'

Kate lifted her head. 'Why?' she asked.

He kissed the vulnerable spot where her hair met her temple. 'The other night,' he said curtly, 'was it the first time since—since you conceived Nick?'

At her nod he went on, 'I tried to be gentle, but I made no concessions.'

Her heart started to jump. 'Neither did I,' she said stoutly, kissing along his jaw, lips tingling at the raw silken texture of his skin. 'It was wonderful because it was you. I'm not made of cotton wool, Patric. I love you and I want to make love with you. What happened with Sean was horrible, but it has nothing to do with us.'

His arms tightened. 'God, I love you,' he said, and kissed her, pressing her back into the pillow.

And what started with restraint ended in wildfire intensity, in untamed, exquisite fulfilment.

EPILOGUE

'OH, IT'S so hot!' Kate took off her hat and exhaled heavily.

'It *is* summer,' Patric said from behind her.

Laughing, she turned to kiss him. He returned it with interest and enthusiasm.

'Why do you do that all the time?' Nick asked teasingly, emerging from his bedroom, the same room Kate and he had shared the night they'd come back from Australia—only four months ago! 'When I grow up and get married will I have to kiss the lady all the time like you do?'

'Almost certainly,' Patric said, smoothing Kate's thick hair back from her face, 'but you'll find it feels good.'

'I don't think so,' Nick said cheerfully. 'Did you find us a house, Mummy?'

'I might have,' Kate said, resting her head a moment on Patric's broad chest before pulling away. 'The agent said she has a glorious place overlooking a tiny private beach on the North Shore. It has a jetty and a mooring.' She smiled at Patric. He had decided to change the sleek racing craft he already owned for something more suited to cruising holidays with a family. 'Are we interested?'

'I am.' But Patric sounded non-committal. 'What about you?'

'We can view it tomorrow morning at ten. Will that be all right?'

'Very,' he said.

Kate gave him a keen glance. Although she was getting better at reading his face, he'd reverted back to the poker-faced man who'd wooed her and caught her in the silken nets of love.

Tension plucked at her nerves, but she had a confidence now that she hadn't had then. He would tell her when he was ready.

He waited until after Nick had gone to bed. Then he sat down beside her on the big sofa in the sitting room and said, 'Brian Pierce rang me today.'

Kate looked up sharply. Brian Pierce was the specialist who'd conducted the DNA testing. She reached for Patric's hand. It had happened; now he had to say goodbye to the last particle of hope that Nick might not be Sean's son.

Patric's hand twisted, clasped hers. 'It's a perfect match. Kate, Nick is my son.'

Kate's mouth dropped open. 'I had a period,' she said numbly. 'Between when we made love and—and Sean. I had a period—a proper one. Nick can't be yours...'

He lifted her hand and kissed it, holding it to his mouth as he said, 'Was it lighter than normal?'

'I—yes. Yes, I think it was. But it was a proper period.'

Very gently he said, 'Brian consulted a gynaecologist. She said it can happen like that—you get what appears to be a lighter period, but it's really the fertilised ovum embedding itself.'

Dread suddenly vanished from the hidden reaches of Kate's heart. She whispered, 'Oh, thank God. Thank God. I used to pretend—and now it's true.'

'Darling Kate, don't cry.' He gathered her into his arms, holding her close while the storm of weeping shook her. When she'd choked back the last sobs he tipped her chin, looking into her face.

'It wouldn't have mattered,' he said, so decisively that she blinked. 'Of course I'm delighted, because this means that Sean hasn't any sort of claim, but Kate, I told you I'd never allow him to shadow Nick's life.'

Kate bowed her head into her hands. 'I don't deserve you,' she said shakily.

'You don't deserve someone who thought you'd lied about being raped?' He spoke with raw self-contempt.

'Who cold-bloodedly set out to woo you so that I could get my son? I even organised the upgrade to first class on the way back from Australia so that my son would be more comfortable. I lied, Kate.'

'And I didn't tell you that Sean was Nick's father. I lied about the man who stole the car. It doesn't matter,' she said, lifting her head. 'You know it doesn't matter now.'

His expression lightened. 'We'll make those lies up to each other. We had to wait a long time, you and I, but it's been worth it for me.' His voice was deep and sure, rich with love.

'And for me,' she said, hugging his hand to her breast. 'It was *all* worth it, Patric.'

'Sweet Kate,' he said huskily, 'my treasure, my dearest girl, let's leave it behind us now.'

'Yes.' She pulled his head down and they kissed, a kiss that closed the door on the past and opened one into a future more filled with joy and happiness than Kate had ever hoped for. That future stretched out in front of them, a shining, wide path. All they had to do was step out onto it without looking back.

And it was suddenly so simple to do.

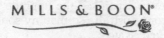

MILLS & BOON®

Next Month's Romance Titles

♡

Each month you can choose from a wide variety of romance novels from Mills & Boon®. Below are the new titles to look out for next month from the Presents™ and Enchanted™ series.

Presents™

LOVER BY DECEPTION	Penny Jordan
THE SECRET MISTRESS	Emma Darcy
HAVING HIS BABIES	Lindsay Armstrong
ONE HUSBAND REQUIRED!	Sharon Kendrick
THE MARRIAGE QUEST	Helen Brooks
THE SEDUCTION BID	Amanda Browning
THE MILLIONAIRE'S CHILD	Susanne McCarthy
SHOTGUN WEDDING	Alexandra Sellers

Enchanted™

A NINE-TO-FIVE AFFAIR	Jessica Steele
LONE STAR BABY	Debbie Macomber
THE TYCOON'S BABY	Leigh Michaels
DATING HER BOSS	Liz Fielding
BRIDEGROOM ON LOAN	Emma Richmond
BABY WISHES AND BACHELOR KISSES	Valerie Parv
THERE GOES THE BRIDE	Renee Roszel
DADDY WOKE UP MARRIED	Julianna Morris

On sale from 4th June 1999

H1 9905

Available at most branches of WH Smith, Tesco, Asda, Martins, Borders, Easons, Volume One/James Thin and most good paperback bookshops

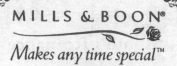

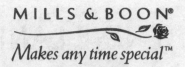

FREE!

4 Books
and a surprise gift!

We would like to take this opportunity to thank you for reading this Mills & Boon® book by offering you the chance to take FOUR more specially selected titles from the Presents™ series absolutely FREE! We're also making this offer to introduce you to the benefits of the Reader Service™—

- ★ FREE home delivery
- ★ FREE gifts and competitions
- ★ FREE monthly Newsletter
- ★ Books available before they're in the shops
- ★ Exclusive Reader Service discounts

Accepting these FREE books and gift places you under no obligation to buy; you may cancel at any time, even after receiving your free shipment. Simply complete your details below and return the entire page to the address below. *You don't even need a stamp!*

YES! Please send me 4 free Presents books and a surprise gift. I understand that unless you hear from me, I will receive 6 superb new titles every month for just £2.40 each, postage and packing free. I am under no obligation to purchase any books and may cancel my subscription at any time. The free books and gift will be mine to keep in any case.

P9EB

Ms/Mrs/Miss/Mr ....Initials ....
BLOCK CAPITALS PLEASE

Surname...

Address..

....

....Postcode ....

Send this whole page to:
THE READER SERVICE, FREEPOST CN81, CROYDON, CR9 3WZ
(Eire readers please send coupon to: P.O. Box 4546, DUBLIN 24.)

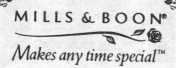